PUFFIN BOOKS
Editor: Kaye Webb

SAM PIG GOES TO THE SEASIDE

'What's the sea like, Brock?' asked Sam Pig one day.
'It's water, going on for miles and miles, and years
and years,' said Brock. 'The sea is alive and it makes
a noise like the wind in the forest. It roars like
thunder and then it sighs like a little tired animal.'

'I should like to go and see it,' said Sam Pig, but
he couldn't walk all the way and Sally the mare and
Farmer Greensleeves wouldn't take him. So in the
end it was Molly the dairy-maid who arranged for
him to go in the bus with the Old People's outing!

'Very ugly,' said some of the Old People, staring
hard at Sam and his sister Ann, but they were much
too busy building palaces in the sand, talking with
flocks of sea birds and listening to their new mermaid
friend playing her golden harp to be at all bothered
by them.

That is just one of the stories in this book, but all
the adventures of this cheerful, kindly, hopeful
little pig have the same airy, country magic, whether
he takes his first spin on a bicycle, hatches out a
golden goose, plays an unlucky trick on the Fox,
or takes a little lost boy home with him to feed on
roast potatoes.

Alison Uttley is one of the best-loved English
children's writers of this century, and we are pleased
to offer so many of her other titles in Puffins:
*Adventures of Sam Pig, Yours Ever, Sam Pig, Little Red
Fox, More Little Red Fox Stories, Magic in My Pocket,*
and two for rather older readers, *A Traveller in Time*
and *The Country Child.*

Alison Uttley

Sam Pig Goes to the Seaside

Sixteen stories of Sam Pig

Illustrated by A. E. Kennedy

Puffin Books
in association with Faber and Faber

Puffin Books, Penguin Books Ltd,
Harmondsworth, Middlesex, England
Penguin Books, 625 Madison Avenue,
New York, New York 10022, U.S.A.
Penguin Books Australia Ltd,
Ringwood, Victoria, Australia
Penguin Books Canada Ltd,
2801 John Street, Markham, Ontario, Canada L3R 1B4
Penguin Books (N.Z.) Ltd,
182–190 Wairau Road, Auckland 10, New Zealand

First published by Faber and Faber 1960
Published in Puffin Books 1978

Made and printed in Great Britain by
Richard Clay (The Chaucer Press) Ltd, Bungay, Suffolk
Set in Monotype Baskerville

Contents

Rags and Bones

'Any rags or bones or bottles?' sang a weary voice. Sam ran to the hedge and looked through. There was an old tramp marching down the lane, singing to himself before he got to the village. 'Rags, bones or bottles,' sang the voice again, and Sam was delighted.

'Yes,' he squeaked. 'Yes, there's Badger's bottle of embrocation. There's only the smell left now.'

'Any bones?' asked the beggar, staring at the little pig whose ears were hidden by the greenery.

'Only in me,' sighed Sam.

'Any rags?' asked the beggar.

'There's my torn trousers,' added Sam. 'Shall I get them?'

The beggar nodded; he pulled out a dirty pipe and sat down in the lane to wait while Sam fetched his goods.

Sam bustled back to the house calling 'Any rags, bones or bottles?' as he flung open the door.

He seized the embrocation bottle and the old pair of trousers, and Ann's bonnet and Tom's scarf and

Badger's old coat. Then, before Ann could stop him, he raced away.

'Now what has Sam done?' wondered Ann. 'I like my old bonnet and Brock loves that old coat. I must follow and watch Sam. Perhaps he has gone to clothe a scarecrow.' She ran off, across the field into the lane, where she heard voices.

'Hi, Mister,' called Sam. 'Here's some good stuff for you. What will you give me?'

The beggar was eating a crust of bread with some cheese; his clothes were old and tousled and he was rather like Brock the Badger himself. His hat was green and crumpled, his hair was shaggy and rough, brindled with white, twined with bits of straw and grass.

'Hello,' said the beggar, when he saw Sam out in the open. 'So you're a pigling, are you? I thought your voice was a bit squeaky. Come and sit along of me and show me what you've got, for I've never traded with a pigling before.'

He took Brock's green, old, stone bottle and removed the straw cork. He took a good sniff and then another. A wonderful country smell was there and he sniffed again.

'This is grand,' said he. 'It has cured my headache already, and I think it will cure my heartache, too. I feel merry as a cricket.'

He sniffed once more and then he nodded his old head.

'Yes, I'll take this bottle. I can make my fortune with this, for all the folk on earth have heartaches. What would you like in exchange?'

Sam hesitated. There were so many things he wanted, yet sometimes he felt that he already possessed everything in the world.

'A saucepan for Ann,' said he. 'Ann wants a saucepan to do our cooking, for Tom won't lend his.'

The beggar felt in his sack and brought out a bent saucepan with an iron handle. The pan was made of brass and it was green with verdegris and black with neglect.

'Will this suit you? It's a good old pan, and it will cook many a meal but people don't like copper and brass pans nowadays. Too much cleaning for the lazy ones. So this was thrown away and I picked it up.'

'It's a lovely pan,' stammered Sam, and little Ann cooed as she looked through the hedge. Sam was a kind brother. Her heart beat excitedly as she watched Sam and the beggar-man. A starling sang a shrill song and a blackbird hopped near and flirted its tail, as it looked at the saucepan. It was indeed a good old pan.

'You must clean it with a bit of grass and polish it with sand,' said the beggar. 'This green on it is poison, so keep this old pan as clean as – as – ' He looked around him and then stared at the blue sky. 'As clean as the bright sun,' he added.

So Sam at once gathered a fistful of grass and wiped the pan, and he polished it with some sand from the lane till it shone like the sun.

'Oh-oo-oo-oo-oo,' murmured little Ann through the hedge.

'Now what about this old coat of Badger's?' said Sam, spreading out the old worn coat. The beggar-man stood up and threw off his own ragged coat. He tried on the Badger's. Although it looked too small, it fitted him perfectly and suited him admirably. He strutted up and down.

'No,' squeaked Ann from the hedge. 'Brock loves that coat. You mustn't sell it, Sam.'

'Sorry,' said the beggar-man. 'Sorry. I quite agree with that voice. The coat gives me strange, wild feelings such as I shouldn't have. It makes me want to live in the deep woods, it makes me hate mankind. It makes me fierce and I want to dig for roots and climb for honeycomb and do all manner of strange things. No, I won't take this old coat, for it's got some magic in it, I think.' He removed it and put on his own coat.

'All right,' said Sam, and he thrust Badger's coat into the hedge. 'It's Brock's special old coat which he wears when he goes hunting in the deep woods and doesn't want anyone to see him.'

Then he showed the beggar-man his own old trousers and Ann's bonnet and Tom's scarf.

'I'll buy these,' said the beggar-man and he put

the bonnet on his head, so that Ann laughed. He removed it and stroked it and fondled the ribbon. Then he touched Sam's old trousers and these he put in his sack together with Tom's ragged scarf.

He fetched out a straw bonnet with ribbons and bits of lace and a red silk rose, old-fashioned and worn, in the place of Ann's bonnet. Ann gasped with delight as she saw this headdress which had belonged to a pretty girl of a hundred years ago.

He offered Sam a woollen vest instead of the trousers and a handkerchief for the scarf. Sam was well satisfied and he tucked the goods under his arm and began to say goodbye.

'Meet me again when you've anything to sell, young pigling,' said the beggar-man and he rose to his feet and walked away very content. For he had an ancient bottle which would cure every ill and give health to all who took a sniff. He had a scarf made of fine cobwebs, such as a lady might wear if it were cleaned and dyed, for no mortal loom had woven it. He had a pair of little trousers with holes like lace, darned by Ann with curious stitchery and patched with colours of the woodland, and he had a bonnet of strange design which he might sell to a museum, for nobody had ever seen the like.

Sam and Ann Pig ran home excited and happy with their share of the exchange. The bonnet suited Ann, she looked quite pretty with the red rose and the green ribbons and the quilted lining. The vest

would keep Sam warm in winter and he didn't mind the holes. Ann washed it and scrubbed it and then darned it with fine pig-stitches, which made the lacy design of leaves and flowers and cobwebs the beggar had admired so much. The handkerchief was a present for Brock, for it had a picture of London with the Houses of Parliament on it and a hole in the River Thames. As for the saucepan, when they had cleaned it again and polished it until it was as new as it was in Tudor days, they cooked the supper in it. The most delicious smell came from it and a most wonderful taste was in the food. Bread and milk tasted of honey and roses. Soup tasted of herbs and wine and sunshine. Mushrooms tasted like a fairy food. It was a magical saucepan which could make a feast from the simplest ingredients.

The old beggar-man made a fortune with his empty bottle. He set up as a quack doctor who could cure every ill, and people flocked to him every day. They went from his room smiling and well, cured of their heart sickness, filled with a loving kindness which Brock the Badger had left in this old bottle. Only a sniff at a pound a time and they were cured, completely.

Sam Pig Goes to the Seaside

'Have you ever been to the sea, Brock?' asked Sam Pig one day when he and the badger were walking in the woods.

'No, I haven't,' said Brock. 'The sea isn't the place for little pigs or even for badgers.'

'What's it like, Brock?' asked Sam, who was sure Brock knew everything.

'It's water, going on for miles and miles, and years and years,' said Brock.

'Can you fall in and get drowned?' asked Sam.

'You can indeed, Sam. It isn't safe for little pigs. The sea is alive, and it makes a noise like the wind in the forest. It roars like thunder and then it sighs like a tired little animal.'

'I should like to go and see it,' said Sam.

'Not safe, Sam, unless you can get someone to take you there,' said Brock. 'But there's Sally the mare in the field yonder. You ask Sally.'

The badger turned deep into the wood and Sam ran off to talk to his dear friend Sally.

'Hello, Sally,' he cried joyfully, as he climbed

the gate and rubbed his cheek on the warm top bar.

The mare looked up at him. 'Hallo,' said she with a whinney of delight. 'Come along and have a chat. Here I've been talking all day to this old gate and all it can say is:

' "*Sam Pig, Sam Pig, every afternoon
Come and sit along o' me and sing a little tune.*" '

The mare unlatched the gate with her nose, and Sam swung backwards and forwards listening to the lovely squeak of the rusty hinges.

' *Oak gate, meadow gate,
I'll sit along o' you.
I'm weary of my family,
I wants to be with you,*'

sang Sam, and the gate was delighted to have the little pig on its broad oaken back.

'Sally,' said Sam, 'have you ever been to the seaside?'

'Can't say I have, Sam,' said the mare, cautiously. 'Not really to the seaside. I've been to the riverside, and the canalside and the brookside but not the seaside.'

'Oh dear, I do want to know about the seaside,' said Sam.

'Why?' asked Sally. 'I don't want to know about

it myself. There's no grass on the sea and the water's too salt to drink, they say.'

'I want to go there,' said Sam. 'Will you take me, Sally?'

'No,' said Sally, decidedly. 'I'll tell you something about it though, for the family goes every year and when I bring them back from the station I hear all the tales.'

'Does Farmer Greensleeves go?' asked Sam.

'Yes, Sam, and the children take buckets and spades.'

'Do they have to work at the sea?' asked Sam, dolefully.

'They make little sandpies,' said Sally, 'but I don't think they eat them.'

'Then I'm going to ask Farmer Greensleeves to take me,' said Sam.

'He won't do that, Sam. No use asking, for the Missus wouldn't go if you went. She wouldn't be seen with a pig.'

The gate began to sing in a soft, little voice:

'*Sam Pig, Sam Pig, going to the sea,*
Catch a little lobster and bring it home to tea.
Sam Pig, Sam Pig, digging in the sand,
Find a little starfish and bring it back to land.'

'How do you know all this?' asked Sam, surprised.

'I'm the Wishing Gate, Sam. Have you forgotten?

You asked to go to the sea and I expect you will manage it.'

Sam met Molly the dairy-maid and he told her of his wish to go to the sea.

'There's a bus going with the Old People of the village on Monday,' said Molly. 'I wonder if you could slip in among them? Sometimes you look like one of those Old People, and you could wear a shawl or a long coat and a bonnet.'

Sam didn't much like the idea of being an Old One, but then he remembered the old Witch-woman in the cottage who had befriended him once. 'I'll ask her about it,' said he.

The old Witch-woman was alone when Sam called and she was very pleased to see him.

'My little Pigwiggin,' she cried, 'I am delighted to see you again. Come along in and tell me the news.'

'Please, Ma'am, can you help me to go to the sea?' asked Sam. 'Molly says there is an Old People's bus and I might go in it just to get a peep at the sea, 'cos I've never seen it.'

'Well, my little Pigwiggin, I will see what I can do. Those old people want cheering up and you might go as an entertainer. I think I can arrange it. You play the fiddle, don't you? Then I will ask the Vicar if I can take a young musician with me to cheer the old folk with his music.'

'Oh, thank you,' cried Sam, kissing her hand. 'I will go home and practise my music.'

So it was all arranged that Sam should join the old woman on Monday morning with his fiddle and his bucket and spade and fishing net.

'I would like to go, too,' said little Ann Pig.

'Then come along, Ann,' said Sam. 'You could wear that new bonnet from the rag-and-bone man which suits you very well.'

So two little pigs arrived at the Witch-woman's house early on Monday morning. Ann carried Brock's flute and Sam had his fiddle. Sam wore his big hat pulled down over his ears and a muffler round his neck covering his nose. He had his best trousers on, mended and neat, and a coat of Badger's which smothered him with its folds. Ann wore her best dress and her straw bonnet with quilted lining with ribbons and red rose, and on her shoulders was a blue cloak which had been made out of a piece of stuff Mrs Greensleeves had given to Sam.

'You look very nice, my dear,' said the old Witch-woman, whose dress wasn't so grand, either, for it was tucked and flounced and beaded as it had been for fifty years. She wore her rusty black bonnet and mantle and she carried a large bag with sandwiches for all of them.

The Vicar welcomed Sam, but he grumbled a little about Ann. 'No room for children,' said he, 'only for Old People; but you have an old-fashioned look so I will allow you to go with your brother.'

'Thank you, sir,' whispered Ann, who was always

frightened of people, for she didn't understand the
words they used; 'old-fashioned' was something
strange to her. 'Does this mean I look very, very
old?' she asked Sam.

But the bus came up and all the old women looked
out to see the odd trio with the Vicar: the old Witch-
woman in her ancient clothes and the two children.

'My friends,' said the Vicar, as he pushed Sam
and Ann into the bus. 'My dear friends, I am taking
two little orphans – er – er – er – lonely ones, but the
boy can play the fiddle and his sister, I am told, has
a flute to give us a little music on the way. I am sure
you will be very kind to these two little strangers,
who are akin to us although not exactly of our kind.'
He stopped, for he saw Ann's little hoof and her
nose.

'Who are they? Ugly faces!' whispered one
woman. 'The Vicar does take up with some queer
characters. We are all respectable women, and these
gypsy folk are – well, I ask you!'

'Hush!' replied the other woman. 'We are all
equal in the sight of the Lord.'

Sam thought the time had come for some music.
He took out his little fiddle and played a few notes
and he put such magic in it everyone listened; cares
were soothed away and a deep content came over
the wrinkled old faces. Quietly he played as the bus
gathered speed, and his music was the song of the
birds in the air and the river in the hollow; it had

the murmur of the wind through the trees and the
humming of bees in the honeysuckle. Then he
played 'All people that on earth do dwell,' which he
had once heard when he was standing outside the
church among the tombstones. The Vicar stared,
delighted that such a good little creature was on the
bus, although he was not sure of Sam's face. He
dimly remembered a little pig at a Flower Show and
at the Sports, someone who won the prizes. He
remembered that something had happened, but he
was vague about it all.

'My child, what is your name?' he asked, leaning
towards Sam.

'Sam Pig,' replied Sam, demurely.

'I seem to remember you, Sam Pig,' said the
Vicar. 'Were you at the Fête for our Church funds?
Didn't I once give you an ice-cream?'

'Yes, sir,' beamed Sam. 'That was me.'

'Would you like another ice?' stammered the
Vicar. Really, a pig! he thought.

'Oh, yes, sir,' said Sam.

'Then at the first stop I will buy one for you and
the old ladies here. Young and old, we like ices,
don't we, Mrs Ollerenshaw?' said he to an interested old woman who was staring fixedly at Ann's
hoof. Ann quickly drew her foot under her skirt and
blushed. She took out Brock's flute, held it to her
pursed lips, shook the bonnet over her forehead and
began to play. She gave the company the music she

had heard at the Fair, the rollicking tunes of the roundabouts, and Sam played a few cascades to keep her company. They played nursery rhymes and ditties and 'Ol' Man River' which Sam had heard at the Blue Boar when he stood at the door one night listening to the singers within.

The bus stopped, the Vicar alighted and bought ices for the company and Sam and Ann felt as happy as larks. Here they were in good society going to the sea with the Vicar and his friends. Off they went again. 'Can ye play "All things bright and beautiful"?' asked an old woman, humming the tune. Sam nodded. So he played and they all sang 'All things bright and beautiful, All creatures great and small'.

When they arrived at the sea, and Ann saw the people walking along the promenade and piers, and the great stretch of water with the sun shining on it, there was a moment of panic. The little pig was so alarmed she tried to get under the seat of the bus and stay there. Everybody else got out and Ann remained, but Sam and the Witch-woman and the Vicar persuaded her it was quite safe.

'Too many people,' murmured Ann, 'and too much water. I don't like it here.'

'Come along,' whispered Sam. 'We'll play alone.'

'You two take your buckets and spades and amuse yourselves in a quiet spot,' said the Vicar, sympathetically. 'Don't be late, we leave at five o'clock.'

Far away over the sands Sam could see some rocks and he took Ann's hand and ran as fast as he could away from the people to the lonely place on the sand where nobody sat.

'Nervous children,' said one old woman, watching them. 'They run as if they were scared to death. Might never have seen company before.'

'They have never been to the sea,' explained the Witch-woman.

'Who are they and where do they come from?' asked the woman.

'They belong to a very distinguished family called Badger,' said the Witch-woman, haughtily. 'They don't mix with ordinary people.'

'Very ugly, like pigs,' retorted the woman firmly. 'No wonder they don't mix.'

But Sam and Ann were far away. The golden sand was firm under their feet, and nobody followed them. At last they slackened their speed and rested. They were alone with the sea and the sand, the shells and seaweed and little rolling waves. Gulls swooped down and called to them and they answered in the universal language of animals. They were not lonely, they had many friends to meet in this corner of the beach. Razorbills, terns, seagulls, cormorants, sandpipers, the birds flocked down to talk to them, whilst Sam and Ann made castles of shapes never seen before and decorated them with exquisite shells which nobody else had found. The sea rolled in the green and orange ferns. Strands of seaweed adorned the palaces they made, and shells and starfish, sea-urchins and fan shells were discovered and admired.

The two little pigs collected a heap of pebbles to take home, and they threw off their hats and paddled in the sea. Sam kept to the shallow edge of the water and both were wary of the deep, blue sea spread out before them.

'We might get drowned. It's bigger than our river and there's no water-maid to play with us,' said Sam to a great gull that kept them company.

'We have a mermaid,' said the gull. 'I will call her to come and see you.'

He flew out to sea and soon returned with a girl who had a scaly gold tail like a fish. Her narrow pointed face was smiling, and fine, gold hair swept the water.

'Why, you are like our water-maid who lives in our river,' Sam told her.

'She is my cousin,' said the mermaid. 'She is a daughter of the river and I belong to the sea.'

'Sometimes she plays to us on her harp,' said Ann.

'I have a harp, too,' said the mermaid. 'I will play to you.'

She swam out to sea and returned in a few

minutes with a small gold harp. She climbed on a
rock and played such music that even the waves
were still. The clouds hung motionless in the sky and
every creature of sea and air stayed to listen.

'Our water nymph can't play as well as you,' said
Ann Pig.

'But she plays most beautifully,' added Sam,
loyally.

'I am older, and the sea is older and the music of
the sea is stranger,' said the mermaid. 'Sometimes
I play to a great ship and they do not know where
the sound is coming from. You see, I catch the
music of the air and collect it in my harp and then
send it out again. It is there always, waiting for us.'

'How do you catch it?' asked Ann.

'I have a bag,' said the mermaid and she showed
Ann a filmy sheet like a cloud which she threw out
behind her and captured the sounds of the air and
the waters.

'But I want to see your castles,' said the mermaid.
She struggled across the sand and looked intently at
the sandcastles the two animals had made.

'Well done,' said she. 'They're beautiful. I will
give you another shell.' She put her hand to her hair
and took a silver-green shell shaped like a fan which
she placed on the castle wall. Then from her purse
she took a coral branch and stuck it like a scarlet
tree in the garden, and under it she dropped a few
pearls like fallen fruit.

'Take these away with you,' she said to Ann, who knew nothing of the value of these sea treasures. 'Give the pearls to somebody who needs money and take the coral tree home in remembrance of me and the green shell give to a friend.'

Then she looked across the sands and she sighed. 'There's someone coming for you, you must prepare to go back. I must leave you at once. I am sacred to the sea and not to be seen of man.'

Ann kissed the mermaid's hand and Sam kissed her snow-white fingers which were as cold as ice. Then the mermaid shuffled back to the sea and swam away carrying her harp. Ann saw someone start towards them from the beach. There was plenty of time and they collected the pearls and coral tree, the green shell, a lobster and a starfish and some of the shells and pebbles.

They ran singing and calling over the sands to meet the stout Witch-woman who was coming towards them and at the same time a wave came out of the sea and washed away every trace of their castles and shells and the marks of the mermaid's tail and her hands. In the water they could see the mermaid watching them; she waved and they waved back. Then on they ran towards the inhabited beach.

'Time to go home,' said the Witch-woman. 'What have you two been doing all this time? I thought I saw someone with you.'

'Only a mermaid,' said Ann, calmly.

'Well, don't mention her to anyone,' warned the Witch-woman.

'She gave me pearls. Would you like them?' asked Ann.

'I'll take them and put them in the Church collection box,' said the old woman. 'Then the Vicar can sell them for the poor of the parish and he will think it is a miracle.'

'It *is* a miracle,' said Sam, gently.

'The lobster is for Farmer Greensleeves,' said Sam, showing his treasures. 'And I have some shells and pebbles for Dick and Molly the dairy-maid and Mary. I have some seaweed for Sally the mare to hang in her stable to tell the weather and some for Farmer Greensleeves. There are shells and pebbles for Brock and the others. We are very rich.'

'And a coral tree for Brock the Badger,' added Ann Pig.

So they joined the others in the bus and they sat so still nobody noticed them, but the Vicar said, 'I hope you enjoyed yourselves, my dears. You were very good amusing yourselves there. Who was that talking to you? I could see her golden hair shining like a light on the sands.'

'Oh, that was . . . oh, that was . . .' stammered Ann and then she was silent.

'It was a mermaid,' said Sam boldly.

'Dear me,' cried the Vicar. 'Well, the Lord has all kinds of creatures on this good earth. "All

creatures great and small", you and the mermaid.
Yes, I can well believe it. Yes . . . yes . . . Out of the
mouths of babes and sucklings comes the wisdom of
the ages. But keep it to yourselves. The village
people might call it pagan. Yes, a mermaid.' He sat
with a strange look on his face.

They arrived safely at the village green and Sam
and Ann and the Witch-woman got off at the corner
of the lane.

'Good-bye,' they called. 'Thank you for a lovely
holiday.'

'Thank *you*, my children,' said the Vicar. 'Dear
me, what lessons one learns in this life.'

He was even more surprised when he opened the
church collection box and there with three old
pennies lay six beautiful pearls, fresh from the sea,
shining with light and pure as truth and the rainbow
itself.

'A miracle,' said he. 'I believe, yes, I believe they
came from the mermaid. A mermaid has no soul,
they say, so we will have prayers for her. Yes, this
will bring help to many of my old people.'

As for Sam and Ann they took their presents to
all their friends, and Brock said he had never seen
such a piece of coral, for it must have come from the
deep parts of the sea. Molly the dairy-maid put the
lovely green shell like a fan in her box by her bed-
side to bring dreams of the sea.

The Lost Boy

One day Sam Pig was walking in the woods when he came across a little lost boy. Sam could hear the little snuffly noises, and the crackling of sticks, and he went warily, for, of course, it might have been a wolf, or a gamekeeper or even the fox. He peered round the tree and crept softly through the brambles, scratching his legs and tearing his trousers even worse than usual. Then he saw him. There sat the little, lost boy with tears trickling down his cheeks and his wide, blue eyes brimming with water. Sam watched the little boy for a while and tears came to his own eyes in sympathy, but he couldn't cry as easily as little boys cry. He saw the child fumble in his pockets and shake them inside out. Sam was much excited when this happened but all the little boy brought out was a small mouth organ. He put it to his lips and made a short wail of music, then he dropped it on the grass and leaned over like a bundle of misery, sobbing quietly. He put his arms around his head and curled up in a ball, with the mouth organ as a pillow.

How Sam stared! He crept close and squatted by the little boy's side, watching that wet, sleepy face, waiting for the child to awake. Overhead a robin sang, and fluttered its wings and fluffed out its red breast. Then down it hopped to a low bush. It began to sing again and Sam, who, of course, knew the language of birds, listened to the words of the song. It was warbling a carol called 'The Babes in the Wood'.

> ' *These pretty babes went hand in hand,*
> *Went wandering up and down :*
> *But never more could see the man*
> *Approaching from the town.*
> *Their pretty lips with blackberries*
> *Were all besmeared and dyed ;*
> *And when they saw the darksome night*
> *They sat them down and cried.*'

The carol was about two children who were lost long ago and covered with leaves by the robins.

The robin picked a leaf and dropped it on the little boy's face, on his lips which were stained with blackberries just like the boy's in the story. Then it began to drop leaves on Sam Pig.

'Steady on!' exclaimed Sam in a gruff whisper as the leaves fluttered down. 'I'm not a Babe in the Wood, I'm not lost.'

'But this boy is,' sang the robin. 'Help me to cover him with leaves, Sam.'

So Sam and the robin spread a nice quilt of autumn leaves over the little boy to keep him warm.

At last the child stirred in his sleep and stretched out a hand which Sam licked with his own warm tongue. Then he awoke and sat up, shaking the leaves away and staring at Sam Pig.

'Had a good sleep?' asked Sam, kindly.

'Hallo,' said the little boy slowly. 'Who are you? I want to go home.'

'I'll take care of you,' said Sam. He pulled out a dirty handkerchief and wiped the little boy's face, making it even dirtier with the wood ashes and mud.

'There, you look better,' said Sam, admiring him. 'I'm Sam Pig. What's your name?'

'Jack Hickory. My father's a thatcher, and he's been thatching Farmer Greensleeves' haystacks, and I started off home alone. I got losted in the wood. I want to go home to my mammy.'

'Well, come along with me,' said Sam. 'I may be only a small pig, but I'm a bold one. I'm not afraid of foxes or bears. I'll take you home.'

So little Sam Pig trotted over the woodland and little Jack Hickory skipped along beside him. Sam took out his pipe and played a tune and the little boy enjoyed the music.

'My Dad can play a mouth organ,' said he, 'and he can play a tune on a straw, and he can whistle.'

'I can whistle,' said Sam, 'and Brock can play a mouth organ and I can play a fiddle.'

Jack handed his mouth organ to Sam and Sam squeaked up and down trying to make a tune.

'What have you got in that bag?' asked Jack, pointing to the satchel on Sam's back.

Sam hitched the bag round and opened it. 'Half a loaf of new bread and a piece of honeycomb. I always take provisions with me when I am going on adventure. Here, take a bite.' Sam broke off some bread and put a piece of honeycomb on the top and Jack ate it hungrily. They drank some water from the clear stream and as Sam raised his head he saw Brock the Badger looking at him from behind a bush.

'Oh, Brock! Come here and see a little lost boy. I'm bringing him home to us,' cried Sam. Brock came from his shelter and held out his paw to the child and Jack took it and kept it in his own small, warm hand.

'You're like a bear,' he told Brock. 'I'm not afraid of you.'

'No need to be,' said Brock. 'You can come home with us and see where we live. We've never had a boy in our house, yet.'

So the little boy went home with Sam Pig and he liked the house so much he did not want to go away.

'You needn't wash,' said Sam. 'I often don't wash my paws and although Ann, my sister, is very particular she doesn't notice me.'

'I'm glad of that,' said the little boy.

'And you can eat as much as ever you want. Lots

of honeycomb and bread and butter and soup,' added Sam.

'Just what I like,' said the little boy. 'Do you have lollipops and ice-cream?'

'No, only ice-cream in winter when Jack Frost comes to the streams and makes it for us,' said Sam. 'And our lollipops are the sweet stems of blackberry bushes. But you can get your feet wet and it doesn't matter.'

So at night the little boy sat by the fire next to Sam Pig and he ate hot roast potatoes with butter and milk, and he went to bed on straw, wrapped in a blanket, next to Sam on the floor.

In the middle of the night he awoke and he lay listening to the snores all around him. Brock was snoring loudly, like an organ, sitting in his chair, not really asleep, and the four pigs were squeaking and grunting like a chorus of bagpipes. It made the little boy laugh and he turned over and curled up close to Sam.

Brock the Badger waked him the next day. 'Be off, you two little 'uns, and wash yourselves.'

'Wash? Sam said I needn't wash,' protested Jack sleepily.

'But I say you must,' said Brock, sternly. 'Go out and dip your head in the stream and splash your eyes to see well, both of you.'

A very wet little boy came back to the table, for there was no towel by the icy cold stream.

Ann threw a brown straw rag to him and he dried himself as well as possible and rubbed himself with bracken, but Sam leapt about without any towel at all. They dressed quickly and ran hungrily to have breakfast.

Tom Pig had cooked a dish of porridge, and the little boy held out his wooden bowl.

'I have porridge at home,' said he, 'and then I have an egg.'

'No eggs for you here,' said Brock. 'You must eat more porridge. We only have eggs for tea or for birthdays or Christmas.'

'But you can have a mug of milk and some honeycomb and bread,' added Ann, who was sorry for the little boy, so clean and so white and so pretty among the brown sturdy little pigs and Brock the Badger.

'I like a little boy,' said Ann. 'You can have my honeycomb, too,' she added.

'I 'spects my mother and father will come looking for me,' said the little boy.

'They won't find you here,' said Tom. 'This house is invisible when Brock wants it to be. He doesn't like mothers and fathers.'

'We have to live invisibly,' explained Ann, calmly. 'Farmer Greensleeves knows about us but nobody else except animals unless we want them to know.'

'I'll show you the dragon,' said Sam. 'And the water-maid and the river.'

So when the washing-up was done and the beds were made and the straw shaken and the house swept clean and the mat beaten at the door, Sam Pig and Ann with the small boy between them galloped off to the woods. They shouted and laughed as they ran. There lay a great brown stone, covered with moss and lichens, deep in the ferns and forget-me-nots.

Sam leapt on its back and Jack followed him, while Ann stood near stroking the stone and removing some of the greenery and tiny ferns which grew in the cracks.

'Can you feel anything?' whispered Sam.

'No,' said the little boy, softly.

'Can't you feel it breathe?' asked Ann.

The little boy held his breath. His eyes were startled. He stooped to the stone and touched it with timid fingers. Yes, he thought he could feel just the gentlest breath, a slow up-and-down movement, as if the earth itself was breathing.

'It's the dragon. He's asleep,' whispered Sam.

'Can you wake him?' asked Jack.

'No, for he might eat you. He ate a cow the last time he was awake, and he kept us busy trying to feed him,' said Ann.

'Where are his eyes?' asked the boy.

'Here,' said Ann, 'I've been uncovering them.' She showed Jack two narrow slits through which he could see a dark crystalline sparkle. Then a larger slit in the stone seemed to move and a great mouth slowly opened and a set of sharp, brown, stony teeth was shown. The dragon yawned and sent out a puff of smoke blue as the forget-me-nots. Then it snuggled down in the undergrowth so that Sam and the little boy fell off and rolled away. The dragon lay very still, fast asleep.

'Oh, dear, we nearly wakened him,' cried Ann with a tremor.

They ran away, but when they were on the edge of the wood they all turned round. The stone lay very still, the dragon was safe for perhaps a thousand years.

'Now let's go to the river,' said Sam. 'Can you swim?'

'Oh, yes,' cried Jack. 'My father taught me.'

'We can swim, too, but not very well,' said Ann, laughing. 'We'll dive in and look for the water-maiden. She sometimes sits on a rock and plays a little harp.'

'But we have to be quiet or the river won't like it,' added Sam. 'Old Man River gets very fierce with us.'

They undressed and leapt into the rushing river, and swam about the rocks in the pools. It was so clear the little boy could see the bottom and down there he spied a small golden looking-glass. He dropped to the sandy bottom and brought it up.

'Look what I've found,' he cried.

'Oh, it belongs to the water-maid,' said Sam.

They all climbed on the green, mossy rock and the little boy waved the glass to catch the sun rays and reflect them on the water. In a minute there was a ripple beside them, a white arm came out of the water, and the mirror was taken from the child's hand.

'Thank you, O boy,' said a sweet, soft voice, high and clear. There below them was a most beautiful girl, with long gold hair and smiling wet face. She held the mirror and sang a water-song to the little boy and the two pigs.

> *'Water, dreaming water,*
> *Here am I, your daughter.*
> *Shall I bring you morning flowers,*
> *Or fountains clear of golden showers?'*

Tossing spray over them in a fountain of drops, she dived into the waves and disappeared.

'See, she's left something,' said Jack. He picked up a green, silken scarf which floated near and he wound it round his neck.

'I think she left it for you,' said Ann.

But the water began to growl and roar, it threw a wave at them and washed them off the rock. It sent a bigger wave and drove them from the river to the bank.

'Give me back my daughter's scarf,' growled the river, and, frightened by the tumult, Jack tossed it away. 'It is for no earth-child,' said the river.

They ran as fast as they could over the water-meadow back to the woods.

'The river is cross today,' said Ann. 'I thought the scarf was a present to you, Jack. I didn't know. I'm sorry.'

'We got away just in time,' panted Sam Pig. 'I don't think the river likes humans.'

They strolled through the woods and Sam told the little boy about the trees and the berries and the flowers they saw, and they picked a bunch of flowers. Then they heard footsteps and they hid behind a tree.

'Oh, dear, I wish I could be invisible,' sighed Sam. 'I don't want anyone to see us.'

'It's my father,' cried the little boy, excitedly. 'He's looking for me.'

So Sam dodged away into the background of the woods and the little boy ran forward to grasp his father's hand.

'Oh, Jack! Jack! Where have you been? We've been looking everywhere for you,' cried the man, as he grasped his little son.

'Oh, my Dad,' cried Jack. 'Oh, I've been living with the four pigs and Old Brock the Badger, in a little house with a straw roof.'

'You have, have you?' said his father, picking some wet straws out of the little boy's clothes. 'What did you have to eat? Swill?'

'And we had honeycomb and nice bread and

milk,' said Jack. 'And do you know I saw a dragon in the wood and a water-maid in the river.'

'Did ye now!' exclaimed the unbelieving father.

'And I was covered with leaves, just like the tale of "the Babes in the Wood",' continued Jack, skipping along and holding tightly to his father's hand.

'Then you can take me to this pigs' house where you've been stopping,' said his father.

'It's this way,' said the child. Then he stopped, puzzled. 'I can't find it, but there's the dragon.' He pointed out the great stone in the wood.

'That's not a dragon. It's nubbet an old rock,' said his father, and when the little boy pointed out the dragon's eyes and mouth where the ferns had been cleared away, the man would not believe it.

'Here, come along home to your mother. You've been dreaming all this,' said the father.

'I haven't,' said Jack, almost in tears, but he soon forgot his anger as he skipped home.

His mother was more understanding and she listened to his tale of Sam Pig and Brock the Badger.

'You never know,' said she, 'there may be such beings. We don't all of us see everything. Little children have power to see things we have lost, I've heard. I think he has been taken care of by somebody and something, and I am very thankful to Sam Pig.'

Jack took her to the woods the next day and showed her the great stone which he called a dragon.

She noticed the bits of moss and ferns which Ann Pig had removed from the slits and she looked closely at the eyes of the stone beast. One eye sparkled and glittered as it watched her, and she thought she saw a wink.

'Put your hand here, Mummy,' said Jack and she laid her warm hand on the backbone of the stone. Surely she felt a slight movement, a breathing of some ancient animal?

Jack took her to the river and she watched the shining glinting water, and she saw the kingfisher flash his wings and the water rat glide softly in the bank. Then did she see the white arm of the water-maiden for a split second? She felt sure she heard the sweet ripple of the harp.

But she could never find Sam Pig's house although she and Jack hunted for weeks, at all times, among the ferns and the forget-me-nots. It was invisible. Only the little mouth organ lay in the wood, where Jack had dropped it.

The Wedding

Sam Pig stood in the stable, admiring Sally the mare. Sally had a white rose in her bridle and some roses tucked in her collar.

'They've all been to a wedding,' explained Sally, as Sam pointed to the flowers. 'I took the family in the best trap to the church and they all went inside. It was a rare sight. I saw the bride and bridegroom come out and the bride carried a bouquet and . . .'

'What's that? What's a bouquet?' asked Sam.

'It's French for a bunch of flowers,' said Sally. 'She carried a bouquet and Mrs Greensleeves was smiling at her and Mr Greensleeves was throwing confetti and I was smiling, too.'

'What's confetti?' asked Sam.

'It's little horseshoes made of silver-paper, the tiniest horseshoes ever known, Sam. They'd do for a mouse, if another mouse went riding on him, same as a horse.'

'Oh,' said Sam. 'What else?'

'They all went to the Blue Boar for a wedding feast. When they had eaten their meal they came out and got into a car. Somebody fastened a real horse-shoe to the back of it, and don't ask me why because no horse was drawing it.'

'I expect,' said Sam, 'they wanted to remember you, Sally.'

'Then I came home, with Mr Greensleeves driving, and the white roses in my headband and a white ribbon on the whip. So I've been to a wedding.'

Sam stared at the whip with the white ribbon standing in the corner of the stable and he looked again at Sally with all her finery. Then he stood on tip-toes, and Sally bent her head so that he could take one of the roses. Sam went off to the farm kitchen with the rose tucked in his scarf. He tapped at the door; nobody was there so he pushed it open and timidly entered. He was never quite sure how he would be received, for Mrs Greensleeves did not like a pig in the kitchen whereas Mr Greensleeves always smiled when he saw him. He crept under the blue linen frill of the settle and waited there among the boots and shoes. It was warm and comfortable near the fire and there were nice smells from the oven. A mouse joined Sam and began to whisper to him.

'A wedding,' said she, 'they've been to a wedding. Would you like a bit of cake? There's some on the table and I could get you a taste.'

'Why? Isn't it Jemima? The mouse I used to

carry in my pocket?' said Sam, staring at the little creature.

'Yes, it's me. It's Jemima Mouse,' nodded the little mouse, 'but don't mention me. They don't like me very much. All the same, I wore a white frill for the wedding to be in the fashion.' She pulled at a little white frill round her neck.

Then she showed Sam a little silver horseshoe she had picked up from the floor.

'You can keep this, Sam. Take it home to sister Ann.'

She ran up the table leg and nibbled a piece of cake with white icing. She pushed it to the edge of the table and peered over at Sam below.

'Open your mouth, Sam,' she cried, and Sam held out his pink tongue. Neatly she dropped the cake onto it and then down she came. They both retreated under the blue frill of the settle just in time as Mrs Greensleeves came into the kitchen. She picked up the cake suspiciously. 'I do believe,' she murmured, 'that wretched mouse has been nibbling here. Oh, dear, I must get a cat.'

Then she noticed Sam's little hoof protruding from the settle. 'What's that?' she cried, and she hauled out the struggling little pig.

'What are you doing here?' she cried, crossly.

'Please, Missus, I saw Sally and I heard about the wedding and I came to find out,' said Sam, wiping his eyes where a tear had come in his fright.

'Don't cry, Sam,' said Dick Greensleeves. 'Can he have a piece of cake, Mother?'

Mrs Greensleeves cut off a morsel and offered it to Sam. 'I'll take it home to Ann,' said he softly.

'Poor little creature,' said Mrs Greensleeves, looking at the tears which trickled down Sam's cheeks. 'I'm sorry I spoke so sharp to you, but you gave me a shock under the settle like that. It was the last straw for you to appear.'

'I'm glad Sam Pig has come,' said Dick, and he took a circlet of roses which little Mary Greensleeves had worn as bridesmaid and placed it on Sam's head in a rakish manner, so that they all laughed.

'Take it home to little Ann,' said he, and Sam ran through the door out to the yard and away before Mrs Greensleeves could change her mind and ask for it back.

'Where have you been, Sam?' asked Brock, suspiciously, as Sam danced into the kitchen and tiptoed with mocking bow to the family.

'A wreath for Ann to wear for her wedding,' said he. 'And a horseshoe for luck, sent by Jemima Mouse, and a white rose from Sally the Mare. All given to me, Sam, and a bit of cake for Ann.'

'Somebody must wear this,' said Ann, trying on the wreath. 'Who could be married?'

'Not me,' cried Sam, 'not me. I tried my luck

with little Polly Ann, and she wouldn't have me and I wouldn't have her, so that's the end.'

'Let's put them on the statue in the garden of the Big House,' suggested Bill. 'He's made of lead, all dark and warm. He's called Cupid. I heard one of the gardeners talking about him. "I left our bread and cheese down by that Cupid," said he, so I went down and found it and ate it and the Cupid boy didn't mind. In fact he smiled at me, and he was glad I had come and eaten that bread and cheese instead of that silly gardener man. The gardener was very cross when he couldn't find his dinner.'

'Yes, he would like a wedding wreath and a rose,' said Ann, pensively.

'Perhaps he had one long ago when he lived in Italy,' said Brock. 'He's an Italian statue from one of their great gardens.'

'How do you know him, Bill?' asked Sam.

'Oh, I was going through the park one day,' said Bill, 'and I took a short cut across the garden of the Big House. I saw that lead boy by the fountain and I stopped to have a drink of water. He spoke to me. He said, "Come and talk to me sometimes, little pig", but I never go that way now.'

'He's lonely out there with nobody to talk to him,' said Ann. 'I have noticed that people never speak to the statues that live in their gardens. They take no notice of them. Not like us; we talk to everybody and we love everybody.'

'Yes,' said Sam. 'We talk to statues and rabbits and birds and everybody else, but those humans can only speak one kind of talk and that's "Be off. Go away".' He squeaked indignantly.

Brock grunted his agreement. 'They talk to dogs and horses but nobody else,' said he, 'so they miss a lot of fun.'

'Let's go now, before it's dark, then we can see him,' said Sam.

The four little pigs set off with the wreath of roses, the large white rose and the little silvery horseshoe, and this time Brock went with them, for he was curious about the statue.

They went across the fields and over the high road to the gates of the Big House. They waited outside the lodge until the lodge-keeper's back was turned and then they all slipped through. Brock had draped some bracken over their heads to conceal them, and a man turned and stared.

'Bracken moving,' he murmured. 'I can't believe my eyes. There must be something there.' He saw the little legs twinkling very fast as the animals rushed in a bunch up the drive and then turned off down the park towards the lake.

'Some piglings,' said he.

They went on towards the smooth, blue water by whose side stood the dreaming figure of a naked Cupid, a child made of lead who rode astride a dolphin. From the mouth of the fish came a small fountain of water. The four pigs and Brock the Badger stood quietly watching the statue. Its eyes turned to them and a look of recognition came into its face, a glow shone on the leaden cheeks, the lips smiled and the eyes sparkled.

'My friend who once spoke to me,' said he, softly, as he saw Bill Pig. 'Friends come to see me.'

'We've brought you a present,' said Bill.

'A wedding present,' added Sam. 'Can you marry somebody?'

'I will marry the water because it loves me,' said the statue, and he held out his small, curved hand and the water fell over it in a caressing stream.

Then Bill placed the wreath of roses on his leaden curls, and Sam put the white rose in his hand and Ann put the little silver horseshoe on his naked foot. Brock touched the statue and spoke softly to him.

'Blessings on you, fair statue,' said he. 'May you give happiness to all who come here to drink from the spring that flows through your fountain.'

They stayed for a long time talking to him and hearing his tales of magical sights, of the fox at night and the pheasants who came to sip the water and the young people who came now and then from the Big House – once a young housemaid with a village boy, once a young lady of the house with a handsome young man whom she was not allowed to meet. He told of a tired fox which came there for help when the huntsmen were after it and he had shielded it.

He spoke of a hurt swan which came to him for rest and help, and wounded birds which had drunk from the spring.

They heard footsteps in the grass and they silently dived for safety under the blanket of bracken which they had carried. They lay so still the bracken was like a piece of the park with tumbled brown stalks and leaves. A beautiful young girl and her friend walked up to the fountain.

'Oh, look!' cried the girl. 'Even the Cupid has a wedding wreath on this our wedding night. It's a good omen, isn't it? Look at him.'

'How strange,' said the young man, who held her hand.

'No, nothing is strange here,' said the girl with a laugh. 'My grandfather brought this statue from Italy and he said it once guarded an Italian spring and was worshipped by the peasants, who gave it garlands of flowers. Now it guards our spring water and it has a wreath again.'

'I can't imagine English peasants decking a fountain,' said the young man. 'Was it one of the gardeners?'

'I don't think so,' said the girl. 'I think it is a miracle, something unknown and wonderful for us on our wedding day.'

She stooped and kissed the cherub, and then she kissed her companion and they sat down on the rim of the fountain.

'Let's go home,' whispered Brock. So the brown blanket of bracken slowly moved away, so quietly the two never noticed it.

'That was a nice present for the little cherub,' sighed Ann Pig when they got home. 'I shall go again and see him if you will come with me, Sam, to take care of me.'

'Yes, I'll come,' said Sam. 'I'll tell him about Sally the Mare and the way she wore a rose on her head at the wedding.'

Everything Talks

It was a summer's evening and the air was filled with the songs of birds. Nobody listened to them in the house of the four little pigs, for everybody was watching Ann make the tea and listening to the music of tea-making. Even the silver shower of notes from the nightingale was lost in the sounds of the house.

The kettle was calling on the hob, 'I'm boiling, I'm boiling, Hiss! Hiss! I'm ready, Mistress Ann.'

The dresser plates laughed together and Bill took them down and placed them round the table. The bread knife chuckled and squeaked as Tom Pig cut some slices of brown bran-bread and piled them on a wooden dish.

'I'm sharp,' hissed the knife. 'I can cut as fine as a scythe in the meadow mowing the grass.'

'And why?' asked Sam, picking up the knife. 'Because Brock the Badger sharpened you. He's the best sharpener ever was.'

'The edge isn't keen enough,' said Brock, who was listening to this conversation, and he took the

knife and fetched the stone hone from the drawer
and drew it across the blade a few times. A blue light
seemed to shine from the knife as Brock flashed it
through the air, and cut a feather floating in the
wind. 'Now you're really sharp,' said Brock.

Ann was rattling the caddy spoon and measuring
out the herb tea into the big, brown teapot. 'A
spoonful for Sam and one for Tom and one for Bill
and one for me and one for Brock the Badger,' she
sang as she slowly tilted the green herbs into the
pot.

'Hurry up! I'm boiling too fast,' hissed the kettle.

'I'll make the tea,' said Brock. 'The kettle is boiling so fast and the steam might burn you. Look at
the cloud from the spout.'

'I'll burn you. I'll burn everybody,' hissed the
kettle, fiercely sending out hot steam and bubbles of
water. 'I'm boiling. I'm boiling.' It raised its lid and
banged it down with a clatter.

The Badger stumped across the room with the teapot and poured the water into it. 'Bubble, bubble,
bubble,' said the water. 'I was icy cold water from
the spring down in the ground and now I'm boiling
hot water making tea. Hurrah for me! Hurrah for
everybody!'

'There's too much talk in this kitchen,' said Brock
sternly. 'Now be silent, all of you things, and don't
open your mouths until sunrise tomorrow.'

Then the water and the kettle and the fire and the

plates and everything were silent. Sam felt lonely without the familiar hubbub going on around him.

'Brock,' said he. 'Why did you make them all quiet?'

'Because I can't hear myself think,' said Brock. 'I want to listen to the air and the dust and the clouds.'

All was quiet that day and all that night. Brock went out to the woods and he enjoyed the silence and he listened to the invisible ones who floated round him, and he heard the leaves growing and the trees talking and the roots murmuring deep in the earth as they spread out their tendrils and grasped the soil. He heard the stars sing in the sky and the Dog star bark and Orion call to them, as he hunted. He forgot all about his command for silence, as he listened to this conversation in the heavens and under the earth. Then he went home, and the sun had not risen when the little family awoke and got up to make the breakfast.

The clock did not strike because Brock had told it to be silent, but nobody noticed this at first, for, of course, the little pigs were talking faster than ever. The fire was silent, and the flames stopped their small hissing as they licked at the sticks, and the sticks never crackled, they felt too sad, and in a few minutes the fire was dead. Sam poked it and struggled, but never a flame would spring up.

The spiders who had been so busy stayed in their webs and were quiet. They were great talkers, but now never a word. The flies who got caught in the webs got free, for the spiders never heard their cries as they struggled. So away they crawled and the spiders got no breakfast. No wonder they sat gloomily spinning and sighing with no sound. The toad in the garden by the door thought it must be winter. It was so still, he went into his winter quarters and pulled the plants over his doorway and settled down to sleep.

Down came the rain and it was silent rain, with none of its merry patter, and its musical voice never came from the rain-water tub, which caught the water from the roof. The stones upon which it fell were quiet too. They had never had such an experience before, and they were unhappy because they enjoyed the sound of the rain and the hiss of the drops and the voices of nature.

'What has happened?' asked the wind. 'My throat is tight. I cannot rage and roar. I am wounded, I feel ill.' The wind tried to make a noise down the chimneys and among the trees, but there was silence, so in despair it lay down like a vast shape of grey mist which filled the fields and woods. Then everybody said: 'What a great fog has come to us.'

Then grey shapes moved about, and ghosts shook their long thin hands and all the woods were haunted.

The kettle wouldn't boil, the fire wouldn't burn, the knife would not cut the bread. The spring had stopped its song, and the water no longer sparkled as it was lifted from the troughs.

'What's the matter, Ann?' whispered Sam.

'I don't know,' whispered Ann. 'It's too quiet. Not a bird sings, and not a bee hums. Not a rustle or a tinkle or a murmur. No running water. No boiling kettle. No burning fire.'

'Where's Brock?' asked Sam.

Brock opened the door and looked around him.

'Why are you all so quiet?' he asked. 'Where is the breakfast, and where is the fire?'

'Oh, Brock. We don't know,' sobbed Ann.

Then the sun rose and Brock remembered at the same moment as the bright rays of the eastern sun shone into the room.

'Come out, my friends. Let us be happy again,' shouted Brock. 'I was wrong to silence you. I love your voices.'

Then the silence broke, and all the world began to chatter merrily. The nightingale, who had been asleep all night, began to sing its matchless song. The water ran in the spring and Ann filled the kettle. The fire flamed up and licked the sticks, and soon the kettle began to boil.

'I'm boiling. Take me off. I'm boiling,' hissed the kettle, and Brock made the tea.

The dresser plates laughed and clapped their hands. The mugs tinkled and the spoons clucked in the drawer. The bread-knife squeaked as Bill cut a

slice of bread, and the toast sang quietly, 'I'm done. I'm done,' as Ann held it before the fire. The honey-comb hummed with the sound of bees as it remembered its home in the tree, and the work of the bees in the hollow.

'Buzz-buzz,' sang the bees as they gathered the honey. 'We gather sweet gold and it's worth more than money.'

'I'm sharp,' hissed the knife. 'I can cut like the scythe in the meadow,' and they all heard the men mowing at dawn in the fields, and the larks singing their morning hymn and the cocks crowing. All was right with the world again.

Sam Pig Rides a Bicycle

It was a warm spring day and Sam Pig sat on the wall by the side of the road watching the traffic go past. He was partly hidden by an overhanging elder tree, and he sniffed the heavy scent of the leaves and he tasted the white flowers as he waited.

He felt happy and comfortable, with never a care in the world, for he had escaped from his brothers and he was free till hunger made him return home. Then he heard a faint squeal of excitement and a patter of feet. Sister Ann climbed up by his side.

'Let me look, too, Sam,' she begged. 'I want to see the sights. It's quiet at home and – oh, my! Look at that!'

She nearly pulled Sam over as she suddenly grabbed him, and for a moment the two little pigs swayed and swung until Sam got his balance.

Down below, unconscious of the commotion he was causing, a little boy rode along the road on a new bicycle.

The two little pigs watched him. It was Dick Greensleeves from the farm. He pedalled along swiftly, he lifted his legs and rode without touching the pedals. He pedalled again and folded his arms. He swayed violently towards the wall and just in time seized the handlebars again and went on, whistling merrily.

'He's got a new bicycle,' whispered Ann.

'He's had a birthday,' explained Sam. 'Sally the Mare told me about his presents.'

'Oh, my!' whispered Ann. 'How it shines and sparkles, like running water in the brook.'

'I wish –' muttered Sam.

'I wish you had a bicycle, Sam,' said Ann, loyally. 'You could ride it, I'm sure. It looks so easy.'

Sam wasn't so sure, but he wanted to try. Then Dick swung against the wall, and this time he did not balance, and off he fell. The bicycle spun round and lay on the bank, and little Dick groaned in the dust.

'Oh, my leg!' he cried. 'I've scratched all the skin off and hurt my bicycle too. Oh. Oh.'

Sam Pig rushed to help him. 'Oh, it's only you, Sam Pig,' murmured the boy.

Sam picked up the bicycle and leaned it against the wall. A tremor ran through his veins as he touched the cold sweet metal, and smelled the soft warm rubber tyres. Then he stooped over Dick. He washed his wounds and scratches with water from a spring nearby, and he bound them with dock leaves to keep them clean and cool.

'I can hobble home, I think,' moaned Dick, rising slowly to his feet. 'You take care of my bike, Sam. I'll send somebody for it later on. Take care, it's brand new.'

He hopped away, limping and resting, and whistling to keep back the tears.

Sam Pig held the bicycle. He turned it round and the wheels obeyed him. He touched it all over, and something of Sam seemed to go into the bicycle, some animal power went to the machine, and something of the bicycle entered Sam, a feeling for metal and rubber and smooth bearings.

Ann Pig joined her brother.

'You hold it and I'll try,' said Sam in a low trembling voice. Ann held the machine and he climbed on the seat. His legs were stiff, he could just reach the pedals. He held the handlebars with a firm grasp, and suddenly Ann gave a push, and sent him wobbling away.

His little feet lost the pedals, his legs stuck straight out, but he was on a slight slope, and the bicycle went on. Then he found his balance, and his feet touched the pedals, and behold he was riding! It was wonderful. He had never felt so happy. The wheels whirled round, his fat little legs went up and down, his body swayed and swung, but he kept upright and did not fall. Ann ran after him, but she had to stop, he was too fast for her short legs.

Sam came to a corner and swung round into the

road. He met a horse and cart, but he knew the right side and he passed them easily. The man did not notice the small pig in his flopping hat, but the horse shied and shivered as Sam went by.

'Yes, it's me, riding a bike,' squeaked Sam. He knew the horse, a friend of Sally's. How Sam wished to show the mare his fine bicycle, but he knew he could never ride across a rough field. In fact, he could not get off, so he had to go on wherever the bicycle took him.

He rode through the village, and what a commotion he caused! The hens and cocks, the geese and ganders, and all the cats and dogs and little boys and girls saw a fat little pig riding a new bicycle down the road between the cottages.

'It's Sam Pig,' screamed the geese and ganders, but the children cried, 'A Pig! A Pig, escaped from a circus!' and they ran indoors to tell their mothers.

The policeman saw him coming, but he knew Sam very well.

'Now, Sam Pig! What are you adoing?' he called. 'Whose bicycle is that? You're riding to the danger of the public. Too fast, Sam. Put on your brake.'

'Can't,' cried Sam, whose eyes were starting with fright. 'Don't know where the brake is.'

He flew past the blacksmith's shop. Little Polly Ann was standing at the door of her father's forge. Her golden curls shone in the sunlight as she idly

played with her skipping rope. Then she heard the
noise and saw Sam careering down the street.

'It's that little pig who came to school and I
played with him,' she called to her father. 'See the
little pig riding a bicycle, Father.'

The blacksmith stared and left his forge. But at
the door of the forge stood Sally the Mare, waiting
for her turn to have new shoes. She heard the commotion and she turned her great head.

'It's our Sam,' she whinnied. 'Hi, there! That's
young Dick's bicycle, Sam.'

'Yes,' cried Sam. 'I'm taking it back to him. I
can't get off, Sally. Goodbye for ever.'

On he went, dodging everybody, leaving the
bicycle to go its own way, just as a horse finds its way
home. He could not control it. At last he left the
village behind and went along the well-known farm
lane. It was very bumpy, and Sam was shot up and
then dropped down, but he kept his hands on the
handlebars. He steered through the big gate into
the farmyard, and there was Dick talking to his
father.

'Yes, I left my bike in the lane,' said Dick. 'Oh,
here it is,' and he sprang up to see Sam, who shot
over the handlebars and dropped at Dick's feet.

'I've brought it back, Master Dick,' cried Sam,
as he wiped his face, and he pulled his ear in token
of respect and then lifted the bicycle to the side of
the pump.

'Well, I never,' said startled Mr Greensleeves. 'You would do for a circus, Sam, riding like that.'

'Yes, master,' said Sam humbly. 'You see, I couldn't get off. But I shan't go to a circus because of Sally and Brock and you.'

'Well, thank you, Sam,' said Dick. 'If ever you want a ride I'll let you have my bike for half an hour.'

'I've had enough, Master Dick. I've had my ride, but I prefer the back of Sally the Mare. I asked this bicycle to stop, but it went on. I said, "Whoa," and it didn't stop.'

'Well, it came home,' laughed Dick. 'So thank you for bringing it here.'

'I've got a few apples for you to take home with you,' said Mrs Greensleeves. 'You helped our Dick, and his scratches and bruises don't show at all. He is all right after your doctoring.'

'Brock taught me that,' said Sam, blushing.

So home he went, very proud and happy, with a basket full of rosy apples, to tell Brock and his brothers and Ann about his adventures.

Sam Pig and the Fox

One day Sam Pig saw a reddish hump in the woods, so he crept up softly, and what do you think it was? It was the Fox fast asleep. So Sam Pig sat down by his side and thought for a while. Then he got up and whispered in the Fox's left ear.

'Mr Fox, Mr Fox. There's a cock pheasant roosting in the honeybee's tree.'

And the Fox smiled in his sleep.

Then Sam Pig whispered in the Fox's other ear.

'Mr Fox, Mr Fox. There's a stuffed turkey ready cooked in Sam Pig's woodshed.' And the Fox smiled even more.

Then little Sam Pig ran home.

'The Fox is coming to dinner with us,' said Sam.

'My goodness!' cried Ann. 'We don't want that Fox in our house.'

'Oh, he won't have dinner with us; he'll have it in the woodshed,' said Sam.

So Ann stitched up a bag and stuck it with some turkey feathers. Then they filled it with pebbles and laid it carefully on the woodshed floor.

Then the Fox came galloping softly up to the house of the four little pigs and he knocked at the door. Tat-tat-tat.

'Dinner in the woodshed,' called Sam Pig.

The Fox went to the woodshed and at once he found the bag. He began to devour it, removing some of the turkey feathers first. Quickly he tasted the pebbles, but he pretended he was enjoying the feast.

'How are you getting on, Mr Fox?' asked Sam.

'A very nice dinner, thank you, Sam,' said the Fox politely, and he put the pebbles in his pockets and went on pulling the bag to pieces.

Sam was puzzled. 'I hope there are not too many hard bones for you?' he asked.

'I like bones, and there are plenty here,' replied the Fox. Then at last he said, 'Thank you very much, Sam Pig. A beautiful dinner of turkey,' and he set off for home. He was inwardly fuming and he tried to think of a revenge on Sam.

'I'll play a trick on that Sam Pig who thinks he is so clever,' he muttered. 'I'll get even with him.'

Up in the hollow of an oak tree an owl was snoring, and smiling at the Fox. The trees gently waved to and fro, rocking themselves to sleep. Then a nightingale began to sing and the Fox dimly felt the music in his brain. He went home hungry, but not unhappy, as he felt the quiet of the woods and the peaceful music of the birds.

The next morning early he set off, and the doves were calling to one another, 'Coo-roo, Coo-roo.'

> *'We see a Fox all shining red,*
> *Surely he never went to bed;*
> *He looks so fresh and brushed and neat,*
> *He has such dainty treading feet.'*

The Fox's red-gold hair stood on end to let the early breeze go through to his skin. He felt well and happy, and he forgot all about Sam.

Unfortunately Sam himself came tripping along, whistling a song and holding his ears erect to catch the sunshine. The Fox bristled and remembered and plotted.

'Thank you for a nice dinner, Sam,' said the Fox, and Sam half smiled, feeling rather worried at this pleasant manner. Perhaps the Fox could eat stones after all. One never knew with a Fox, he had such strong teeth, thought Sam.

'I was looking down the well at the farm,' went on the Fox. 'Have you ever seen down it?'

'Not really,' replied Sam, 'but I once had some cold water from it.'

'There's a beautiful young pig down there,' said the Fox. 'She lives at the bottom. The farmer keeps her there,' went on the Fox.

'Really? A pig down the well?' cried Sam, astonished.

'Yes, she is waiting for a young prince to rescue her,' said the Fox. 'Would you like to be that prince? Would you like to see her?'

'Oh yes,' cried Sam, eagerly.

'Then follow me now,' said the Fox. So away they went, the innocent little pink Pig, and the wily red Fox, and they walked through the common, keeping to the bushes and edges, and they went over the fields, to the farmhouse. The well was in the corner of the orchard, away from the house, and there was a wooden lid over the top.

The Fox pushed the lid away, and looked down the well at the round mirror of light at the bottom. He could see his own red head and sharp nose reflected in the circle of water at the bottom. The bucket lay on the grass and he fastened it to the rope. At the same time he snatched a red rose from a bush growing near, from a rose tree which had been banished to the orchard ground. He hid the rose behind his back.

'Come and look, Sam,' said he, and Sam leaned over the rim of the well and stared timidly down into the depths. Of course he saw his own little face, but the light of the early morning sun and the radiance of the day made his face shine, and the Fox held the red rose close to his ear. He did not recognize himself.

'Can you see her?' asked the Fox.

'Oh yes. There's a pretty little pig down there

looking at me, and she has a red rose in her hair,' said Sam.

The fox hid the rose as Sam turned his head, and climbed down from the well's rim.

'She is a princess,' said the Fox. 'She is waiting for somebody brave like you, Sam. Dare you go? I wish I were young and nimble and slender like you. I would go myself.'

'Oh, let me go,' cried Sam. 'I will rescue her and take her home to Brock the Badger to live with us.'

He waited for the Fox to sling the bucket over the water and then he climbed inside, squeezing himself into the small bucket with care. The Fox slowly lowered him down the well, and when the bucket reached the bottom he left it there.

'Well, I'll leave you to talk to her, Sam. When you are ready just pull the rope and holler out. I hope you will enjoy your dinner down there in such fine company.'

He laughed and tossed the rose down the well and then he danced away home.

Down in the well little Sam looked round for the princess. There was nobody, but the rose floated on the water. He sat in the bucket and talked to the princess. 'Here am I, little Sam, come to rescue your highness,' said he, but nobody came.

'There's only me down here,' said a fat Toad. 'I live here, but there's no princess.'

Sam started, he called again, then he gave a tug

to the rope, but nobody answered. Then he realized he had been tricked.

'Sam Pig,' said the Toad. 'How came you to trust that old Fox? He's full of tricks.'

'Oh dear,' groaned Sam. 'I thought I saw her down here with a rose in her hair.'

'It must have been yourself you saw, Sam. The light can be as tricky as a Fox, with its reflections and refractions. You will have to stay down here till somebody comes from the farm for water, but they don't often use this well.'

So Sam stayed down at the bottom of the well, and soon he forgot his annoyance in the pleasure he found down there. The Toad showed him many treasures. There were pennies and silver coins which people had thrown down to bring them luck, and Sam put a few in his pocket. There were some needles, for those too are thrown down wells, and pins which the Toad kept on a mossy pin-cushion. One was a pig with a jewelled head, too.

A few lizards and snails and a frog were down there and they came out of their holes to talk to Sam. They told so many tales, that it would fill a book to write them all down. Sam listened, enchanted by their stories of magic down the well.

So there stayed Sam all day, all the lovely summer day, and his family called and called but their voices did not reach him down at the bottom of a well. Sam sat in the bucket, staring up at the bright blue

sky, with dancing white clouds which went across. Then night came and he could see the Great Bear in the sky, and he began to wish to go home. 'Help! Help!' he cried.

At the farm Mrs Greensleeves suddenly felt she would like a drink of cold well water, and Molly went to get it for her. As Molly crossed the orchard she heard that little squeak. 'Help! Help!' She went pale, but she bravely looked down the well and she spied a something white. She turned the handle of the well-head and slowly the bucket came up. It had no water in it, but a fat little pig sat there, rubbing his eyes and half asleep.

'Molly, it's me, Sam Pig,' squeaked Sam, and the bucket swung over the top and out tumbled Sam.

He helped Molly to get some water for Mrs Greensleeves and then they both went back to the farmhouse, where he was feasted on warm bread and milk, and wrapped in a warm blanket.

'So you've been down at the bottom of our well all day,' said Mr Greensleeves. 'You should never trust that Fox.'

'I played a trick on him first,' confessed Sam.

'Then it serves you right,' said the farmer.

Sam put his fist in his pocket and brought out a few trifles to show them. Molly pounced on a silver brooch she had lost. It had fallen from her dress when she leaned over the well one day years before and she had never been able to get it back.

Mr Greensleeves said Sam could keep the money, for he had earned it down there all day.

'Now I must go home,' said Sam. 'They will be looking for me. Thank you very much for the supper; and thank you, Molly, for rescuing me.'

When he arrived home there was a great welcome from his worried family. Brock listened with great interest to his story about the well, and Sam showed him the money which had lain there. Some of the coins were very old, and the needles were thick and ancient, and the pins were made of brass and iron.

'Did you see the Princess?' asked the Fox the next day.

'No,' said Sam. 'I found I was a princess myself. I enjoyed myself, too. There was a kind old Toad, and I got a lot of money and some needles and pins. Molly the dairy-maid invited me to supper so I did very well. Thank you for letting me go down a well, Mr Fox.'

'A pleasure,' murmured the Fox wryly.

'I'm going there again, and I shall take my fiddle and play a tune to that old Toad, for he likes music. I shall play water-music for him.'

'Water-music,' murmured the Fox. 'I can't get the better of that Sam Pig. Whatever is water-music?'

The Golden Goose

It was St Valentine's and Sam Pig sat on the gate of the farmyard, peeping about at the hens clucking in the straw, the cock strutting around, the guinea hens crying 'Go back, go back', and the turkey-cock gobbling, 'Gobble, gobble, gobble'. It was because of the fierce turkey-cock that Sam sat on the gate. The turkey had chased him once and knocked him down with his flapping wings, so Sam kept away from the great bird. The ducks he loved and they talked amiably to everyone as they walked in single file to the pond.

'Quack, quack, quack,' cried Sam, and the ducks nodded and quacked back.

'Gobbly, gobbly, gobbly,' cried Sam, mocking the turkey, and the turkey went very red and stormed at Sam.

The goose and the gander walked proudly round the corner and Sam hissed at them, 'SS-ss-ss-ss', but the couple went through the opposite gate to the further field. Then Sam saw something large and smooth and beautiful, lying in a nest of hay.

'A Valentine egg,' said Sam Pig. He leapt down and held it in his hands. The egg was a delicate yellow in colour but it was rather heavy. Sam hurried off to show it to Molly the dairy-maid.

'Molly,' called Sam. 'Here's a big yellow egg. Would you like it?'

Molly popped her head out of the dairy door.

'A yellow egg? That's a queer-looking thing, Sam. Where did you find it?'

'It's a goose egg,' said Sam.

> '*A good goose will lay*
> *On St Valentine's Day*,'

said Molly, 'that's an old saying.'

She took it from him, felt the weight of it and handed it back.

'No good!' said she.

'Can I have it?' asked Sam.

'Yes, but you can't eat it, Sam. It's a queer egg. That colour's not natural. Throw it away,' said Molly. 'I can't stop now, I'm busy making butter.'

'Molly,' said Sam. 'Who laid this egg?'

'Maybe the "goose that laid the golden egg",' laughed Molly.

'That's what I thought,' said Sam quickly, and away he ran towards home. On the way he had to stop to show the egg to Sally.

The mare was grazing in the meadow but she whinnied when she heard Sam's voice.

'I've got an egg, Sally,' shouted Sam. 'It's the egg of the goose that laid the golden egg.'

'What are you going to do with it?' asked Sally.

'I'm going to hatch it,' said Sam.

'Don't sit on it, Sam. Keep it warm and perhaps you'll have a gosling,' said Sally. 'I've heard of the goose that laid the golden egg, but I never heard of anyone hatching one of those gold eggs.'

'I'm going to hatch it,' said Sam, stubbornly.

When he got home he decided not to tell his brothers and sister about it, they would only mock at him. They would say he was a goose too, and that was why he had a goose egg. They would laugh. No, he wouldn't tell them until the egg hatched out.

He carried the egg upstairs and put it in his warm bed. There it was when he went to bed at night and he cuddled it up and kept it warm and comfortable. He didn't sleep very well, he was afraid of breaking the precious egg.

In the morning he took it downstairs in his coat and carried it to a bed of bracken while he had his breakfast. He was very quiet at breakfast time and the others teased him.

'What plot is he hatching now?' asked Tom, and Sam was startled.

'I'm not hatching a plot. I'm hatching a goose – a goose,' then he stopped and blushed.

'Hatching a goose? Oh, you gander!' sneered Bill.

'Now, little pigs, behave yourselves,' interrupted Brock the Badger, banging on the table. 'Don't call each other names. Geese and ganders don't like to be called pigs, and pigs don't like to be called geese and ganders.'

'Brock,' whispered Sam. 'Brock, I want to speak to you afterwards.'

'Gander!' hissed Bill.

'Goose!' muttered Tom.

Brock took his pipe and filled it with coltsfoot baccy, then he strolled out-of-doors and Sam followed him.

'What's the matter, Sam?' asked Brock.

'I've got an egg, Brock,' said Sam excitedly, 'and I think it was laid by the goose who laid the golden egg. It's gold, Brock.'

'Well, Sam, where is this egg?' asked Brock, looking down at his small companion with twinkling eyes.

Sam showed him the egg wrapped up in a bundle of hay.

'It looks like gold, Sam,' said Brock, 'but it may be pretence, I don't know.'

'I'm hatching it, Brock,' Sam went on.

'I'll give you some fine sheep's wool to put round it,' said Brock and he fetched some silvery wool and draped it in a jacket which kept it warm all day. Sometimes Sam took the egg for a walk inside his coat next to his beating heart. Sometimes he sat and nursed it away in the woods where no one could see him.

The Fox came past one day. He was very much interested in the golden egg.

'I'd love a Golden Goose,' said he, licking his lips. 'I'd give you anything you like for the young gosling when it comes out.'

Sam nodded and smiled and said nothing.

The egg hatched one night and a golden bird came out of the broken shell. In the morning Sam walked downstairs with a golden gosling walking after him.

'Here is my new friend,' said Sam, marching into the kitchen, and the gosling fluttered its golden wings and gave a tiny hiss.

'What a pretty fellow!' cried Ann. 'Where did it come from?'

'I hatched it out of an egg I found,' said Sam proudly. 'I kept it secret except from Brock. It's a goose from a golden egg. I shall call her Valentine, because I found it on St Valentine's Day.'

So Valentine, the golden gosling, came to live in the house with the four pigs and Brock the Badger. The goose had her own little table and feeding bowl in a corner and she ate with the family. She slept in Sam's room in a nest by the side of his bed. She awoke the first and called to him each morning. 'Sam, Sam, wake up. It's a fine day,' she said when the sun shone in the east with golden light like her

own feathers. When the sun was invisible in the clouds and the rain poured down she said, 'Sam, Sam, it's a wet day. You can sleep a little longer.' She didn't mind rain, nor did Sam, and they went out together to get wet, to drink the rain, and to paddle their feet in the pools. She was a rare friend for Sam Pig.

She talked too much for Badger, but Sam enjoyed her conversation. She told strange tales all about her ancestors. They came from Greece, she said, and they lived there when Midas was king. Everything he touched turned to gold. He had touched a goose and she laid a golden egg. Every now and then a goose in this family laid a golden egg and a golden gosling was hatched out.

Sam picked up one of her gold feathers. 'I shall take this to Molly the dairy-maid,' said he. 'She can wear it in her Sunday hat.'

So Molly wore the feather from the golden goose. It seemed to her like a hard, brass feather, she had no idea it was made of gold as she pushed it through the hat-band on Sunday morning.

One day Sam found one of the golden quill feathers from the goose's wing and he carried it carefully, as every little frond was made of the most delicate gold. He sat in the hedge with it, watching the people go past.

'I'll give it to somebody who has the friendly look,' said he to Ann, who sat with him to help him to decide. First came a stout, red-faced man, grumbling all the time, whipping his horse, and shouting at him.

'Not for you, my fine fellow,' said Sam.

Next came a young man driving a car and he went so fast and he frowned so much that Sam did not like him at all. He looked angry when he had to stop a minute to let some sheep go past, and he shouted at the farm-boy who drove them. No, he couldn't have the gold quill.

Next came a woman dressed in fine clothes, but her children looked uncared-for and dirty. She scolded them loudly, and when a child waved to Sam Pig in the hedge she pulled his arm with a jerk.

'Not for you,' said Sam.

So one after another passed, and each was too busy or too cross to deserve a gold quill from the golden goose.

Then Dick Greensleeves rode down the lane on his bicycle and Sam stepped out waving the golden feather.

'It's for you, Master Dick,' called Sam. 'It's to make a pen to do your lessons. It's from my golden goose.'

Dick was delighted and he shaped the quill into a pen-nib and wrote with it when he got home. And the next day he took it to school and all his lessons were correct. Some of the magic of the goose had gone into the feather.

'Where did you pick up this, Dick Greensleeves?'
asked the teacher.

'It's from a golden goose,' said Dick, but he would
not say any more.

'It's pure gold,' said the teacher. 'Take great care
of it, it's valuable.'

Dick would never sell his pen, or use it carelessly.
It was a secret he shared with Sam Pig and it became an heirloom in his family.

As for the golden goose, she stayed with Sam Pig,
his friend and companion. She walked in the woods
with him, for she was safe from any fox with her
feathers of gold to protect her. Brock made her invisible from human eyes and people who saw her at
all thought she was a patch of golden sunshine,
moving among the trees or paddling over the water
with her shadow and Sam.

Sam Pig's Trousers

Little Sam Pig hitched up his trousers and padded swiftly along the lane. Then he saw a gate in the hedge and squeezed under it. Unfortunately he was a little too stout, he had eaten a big breakfast and he stuck fast. He wriggled and squirmed but could get neither in nor out, and there he was imprisoned.

'Oh dear me!' he moaned, 'late again. Tom and Bill will find me and drag me home. Oh dear! I daren't call out. Oh dear! I can hear them coming.'

There was a patter of small hooves in the dust, coming nearer and nearer.

'I tell you he went down here,' said Bill Pig, panting. 'I saw him start down this lane.'

'But he's gone aside in the hedge,' muttered Tom Pig, trotting along behind his brother. 'Our Sam always turns aside. He must be hiding in the hedge.'

Sam Pig could hear their voices coming nearer. He made a desperate struggle and managed to escape but he left behind a piece of his check trousers caught in a nail in the gate. Away he scampered, across the ploughed field, away to the pastures where Sally was grazing. He knew he would be safe there with his old friend the mare.

'Look here, Tom,' cried Bill, 'I told you so. Here's a bit of Sam's red and blue check trousers. Now we have proof. We can't catch him now but we know he came this way.'

'Let's go home, Bill,' said Tom, sitting down in the ditch to scratch himself. 'We'll take this piece of stuff as evidence. I'm tired, running all this way. Let's go home. Ann said there would be dumplings for dinner, barm dumplings with gravy over them.'

'Rich, brown gravy on fat, barm dumplings,' echoed Bill, and he detached the piece of stuff from the gate and carried it like a flag. 'Our Sam will feel a draught with this piece out of his trousers.'

'Serve him right!'

The two brothers walked slowly home to their dumplings and gravy. They placed the checked piece of material on the table and waited for Sam. But Sam didn't come home for a long time, he was enjoying himself with Sally the mare.

With his tail curled in a bow and his nose in the air Sam trotted along. The air was sweet-smelling, the yellow brimstones danced in front of him, the swallows darted overhead. He saw them all but he did not waver from left to right.

He crossed the field to the rich pastures where Sally was grazing, and the smells changed to the warm, rich odours of the farm, of cows and milking, and little pigs and good horses. From the orchard came the delicious scent of apple blossom. A cuckoo called from a sycamore tree. A robin sang on a wild rose spray. Sam Pig danced a little jig of joy and began to sing too.

'Hallo, Sally,' he called, as he climbed over the last gate. He wasn't going to risk squeezing under again.

Sally looked slowly round and stared at the pigling. 'What's happened to your trousers, Sam? You've torn a great piece out.'

'Yes, I know, Sally. I stuck under a gate, that's all,' sighed Sam.

'Well, well, Sam Pig! You must be getting fat, for there's plenty of room under our gates. You used to push under them easily.'

'Yes, Sally, but I'm a little stouter, perhaps. Never mind about the old trousers. I hope they won't find the piece I lost.'

'You'd best get them mended,' said Sally. 'There's a little red hen at the farm. She's a good sewer. And it's washing day, so maybe there's some stuff hanging on the clothes-line in the orchard. You go and see, Sam.'

Sam pranced off to the orchard drying ground. And there hanging on the line were many garments belonging to the Greensleeves' family. Sam stared up but there was nothing that would do. On a low hedge were handkerchiefs spread out to dry and among them he saw a red and blue silk handkerchief belonging to the farmer. Sam neatly removed it, carried it away and went back to Sally.

'This will do, Sally. Where's the little red hen?' he asked.

The little red hen came bustling forward, clucking eagerly. When Sam showed her the hole in his trousers she took a needle-case from under her wing. Then she found a nice, strong thread of hay in the haystack.

'I'll sew it if you'll keep still, Sam,' said she, kindly. So Sam stood very still and the little red hen made a large patch out of Farmer Greensleeves' Sunday handkerchief to cover up the hole. Every now and then a sharp prick of the needle hurt the little pig and he gave a cry but the little red hen took no notice and went on sewing.

'Thank you very much, little red hen,' said Sam when she finished. 'I'll bring you one of Ann's barley cakes tomorrow.'

He climbed on the gate to show Sally, but the mare shook her head at him.

'Farmer won't half be mad when he knows,' said Sally. 'That's his best handkerchief, as he takes to market.'

Sam was rather upset to hear this, so he climbed down and started off home feeling dejected. On the way he met the farmer.

'Hello, Sam Pig,' said Farmer Greensleeves.

'What's that on your trousers? It looks like . . . it fair looks like . . . it much resembles my best pocket handkerchief, Sam.'

Sam blushed and tried to hide the patch but the farmer turned Sam round and had a good stare.

'Yes, it's my handkerchief, a Christmas present from Cousin Martha, and I shall be obliged if you will kindly remove it from your breeches and bring it back to me, safe and sound.'

He walked away in a huff and Sam dithered and shook and blushed again. He went home to Ann Pig and told her the story. She said she would unstitch the patch and put another one on the trousers when Sam had gone to bed. Sam chose a nice piece of stuff from her rag-bag, and then Tom and Bill came in.

'We found this caught on a nail by the gate,' said Bill, holding out a square of stuff.

'Whose is it, Sam?' asked Tom.

'I'm afraid it's mine,' said Sam. 'I must have lost a piece on my way to the farm. I was in a hurry.'

'You missed your dinner,' said Bill. 'It was dumplings and brown gravy.' Sam licked his lips and said nothing.

'You'd best go to bed,' said Tom sternly, so Sam began to take off his clothes. The trousers would not come off. He tugged and something hurt him. Then he knew what had happened.

'I think the little red hen has stitched them to my legs,' said he sadly.

How Tom and Bill laughed, but Ann was sorry for her brother. She took a pair of scissors and cut him free.

Sam rubbed his sore legs with goose-grease ointment, and then he put on his warm pyjamas. He was very glad to get into them and he didn't mind going to bed, for upstairs was the golden goose, waiting to tell him a story.

Ann washed the handkerchief and dried it and ironed it ready for Farmer Greensleeves. Then she patched the trousers with the piece of stuff, and she stitched it with stitches almost as neat as those of the little red hen, but hers made a cobweb like ferns. She called it 'fern-stitch' and it was prettier than herring-bone or feather-stitch which human beings use in their sewing.

Farmer Greensleeves was very glad to get back his clean handkerchief the next day. It was neatly folded into a square and wrapped in a few ferns. With it Sam brought some mushrooms.

'You know where everything grows, Sam,' said the farmer. 'Thank you for these. Now don't you be helping yourself to my clothes. I'll give you a pair of old trousers which you can have cut down for you.'

He fetched a greenish old pair of trousers and gave them to Sam, who started off home with them slung on his back. On the way Sam heard a mournful singing.

'Here am I, all alone, alone – O.
Nobody comes to give me a bone – O.
I'm stiff with pain and cold as stone – O.
Nobody knows I'm here alone – O.
Making my groan, my moaning moan – O.'

'That's Joe Scarecrow,' murmured Sam. 'Oh dear, I'd forgotten him.'

He crept through a gap and there stood the scarecrow, waving his ragged arms and singing his ditty.

'Oh, Sam Pig! I am glad to see you! I've seen nothing but rain and clouds, moon and stars, birds and cows for weeks on end.'

'Isn't that enough?' asked Sam. 'I like those things, Joe.'

Then he noticed the torn trousers with gaping rents through which the weeds were growing. Dandelions bordered the bottom of the trousers and kexes grew tall through the holes.

'Oh, poor old Joe,' cried Sam. 'You do look ragged. I've got a nice pair of trousers here, just given to me. Would you like them?'

'Yes, Sam. They're fine enough for a wedding,' said the scarecrow. 'I'm invited to a wedding next month. Only to watch from the hedge, but that's enough for me. I shall see Farmer Greensleeves drive Sally and the family to the church.'

'Well, you shall have these,' said Sam, generously,

and he helped the old scarecrow to dress in the trousers.

'You look fine and grand,' said Sam. 'You look a fair treat.'

'I feel as rich as a king,' said the scarecrow, and he tossed his arms and scared the birds and sent a kiss to the sun from his straw fingers.

'I'll take your old pair home,' said Sam. He said goodbye to the scarecrow and went away, but from afar he could hear old Joe Scarecrow singing:

> '*O, all you little blacky tops,*
> *Now don't you steal the farmer's crops.*
> *I've got a pair of trousers fine,*
> *So don't come here to sup and dine.*
> *Shuu-uu-uh.*'

'Ann,' Sam cried, as he danced into the house. 'Can you mend these?'

Ann took the old pair and examined them thriftily.

'They must have come from the scarecrow, Sam,' said she.

'That's true,' said Sam. 'I gave him a pair and these are his old ones.'

'I could cut them down for Brock,' said Ann, thoughtfully.

But Brock said they were too ragged for him and he took them out to the woods and gave them to an old badger who lived there. They would do for his bed, and he put them with the bracken and leaves in his holt.

'Thank you,' said the old badger. 'Nice smell in these. They smell of wind and rain and snow. Thank you, Brock.'

Sam up a Tree

It was supper time and Sam Pig lay on the grass half asleep. Bill Pig was busy in the house, Tom was watering the garden with rainwater from the tub, and Ann was mending Brock's coat. There was nothing for Sam to do but to sleep, and to save time he shut his eyes, folded his legs out of Tom's way and sighed comfortably. He was just dropping off into a dream of plum cake and sugar biscuits when he heard the sound of voices very near. He lay quite still, hardly breathing as he listened to the whispering, rustling sounds around him. Very small voices were talking in the grass, close to his ear. The words were so soft that he could only hear them because his head was down on the ground. That's a good place to hear the words of earth creatures.

'Ss-ss-ss-ss,' said something, and he knew it was the talk of the ants. Sam didn't like ants very much because they tickled him.

'Sam-ss-ss. Pig-ig-ig,' said the ants, who always stammer a little if you can hear them properly. 'Ss-ss-Sam Pig-ig-ig can do-do ma-many th-things.

Y-es-es. He is v-v-very clev-er-er, but he can't cl-cl-climb trees. We can go-o-o to the t-tip-t-top of any tree. We can cl-climb u-up and d-down and not fe-feel sick but a p-ig-ig can't cl-cl-climb trees.'

Sam snorted and blew one of the ants away.

'Neither can a pig fly,' said another voice, a quick determined little voice, a buzzing voice, which Sam knew at once was that of a bee.

'I can fly up a tree and stay there,' boasted the bee. 'I can fly through the paths of the air and speed down again without once getting lost. But Sam can't fly.'

Sam Pig had never been a good climber of trees, except nice little apple trees with branches close to the ground. None of the family of pigs could climb trees, and even Brock the Badger was better at digging beneath their roots than clambering among boughs.

'Oh, Brock,' said Sam when he met his friend. 'I wish I could climb trees like Maldy the cat at the farm; she runs up the trunk of the elm tree and looks down at me and puts her tongue out.'

'Now, Sam,' cried Bill, 'you keep on the ground and behave yourself. There's plenty to do, planting potatoes, or weeding, or washing-up, or sweeping the yard without climbing trees.'

'I believe he wants to climb trees so that we can't find him,' added Tom.

'No, I don't,' cried Sam, hotly. 'I want to be high

up and look over the fields and see things. I am only a little pig and I can't see far.'

'I'll give you a leg up, Sam,' said Brock, who was listening. 'I know how you feel.'

So Sam led Brock to a fir tree which was very tall. He stood at the bottom and stared up at the high branches which seemed to touch the sky.

'This tree, please, Brock,' said Sam.

He went close to the tree and stretched his arms up the trunk. Brock gave a heave and up he went to reach a branch, and cling to it. He pulled himself up to sit there. Another bough was near and he went higher and higher, one bough at a time, till he reached the top. It was cold and windy but exciting up there.

'Hello, Brock,' he called. 'I'm at the tip-top. I can see for miles and miles, right to the farm, and there is old Sally eating the grass and she can't see me, hiding in this tree. Oh, Brock, I do like being up here. Can I stay?'

'Yes, if you like, but don't forget you must come down someday,' laughed Brock. 'We shall miss you if you stay there.'

Bill and Tom came to look at their brother in his green nest in the clouds.

'Take care, Sam,' cried Ann, anxiously.

'Silly old Sam,' grunted Bill, and Tom took one look and then went back to the house muttering rude things.

A rook flew to the tree and sat near Sam. That was a great honour and Sam and the rook passed the time of day while the tree gently rocked to and fro like a great pendulum.

'Fine weather,' said Sam, squinting at the sky.

'Aye,' said the rook. 'You can see the sky up here and feel the shape of the wind. Now look yonder to the west. Do you see that little cloud?'

'Yes,' said Sam. 'The shape of a cushion.'

'That's a sign of rain. It will rain when that cloud passes overhead, near this tree-top,' said the rook.

'Sign of rain, Ann,' called Sam. 'Get your washing in.' Ann ran to the little garden and brought in the few rags of clothing which hung on the line between two trees.

The rook cawed and flapped his wings. Then away he flew and a magpie, who had been staring at them, came to the tree.

'Hello, Sam Pig,' said the magpie, and he shook his long tail and balanced on a branch so close to Sam the little pig had to edge away. 'What are you doing up here?'

'Just looking at the view, and watching the clouds,' said Sam.

'Let me warn you, Sam, there's a Fox prowling in the wood over there,' said the magpie. 'I can see a gamekeeper too. I hope he won't think you are a pink bird up a tree.'

'I think he can see you, too,' returned Sam, and

this frightened the bold bird. It rose and flew away with a loud jeering cry, and Sam felt very uncomfortable lest the keeper should really think he was a bird.

Then a cuckoo came to the tree-top, and Sam was mighty glad. It was the first cuckoo, too, freshly arrived from a long journey over the sea.

'Welcome, dear Cuckoo,' said Sam. 'Did you bring Spring with you?'

'Yes, Sam, Spring came flying with me, and now she is up in the air waiting for a warm wind and shower of rain to drop before she touches the ground and primroses and violets will come.'

'I'm very glad,' said Sam. 'I like Spring.'

'There she is, in that warm little cloud which is coming near,' said the cuckoo.

Sam looked up and he saw that the cloud which had been in the west was already coming near. Seated on it, or flying under it, was a fleecy cloudlet, which might have been a girl with long streaming hair, for in her hands she held bunches of little wild flowers, wood anemones, and primroses, cowslips and celandines. They shone in the sun's rays, and sparkled with drops of water on their petals.

'There's Spring herself,' murmured Sam, and he waved a small paw, and Spring dropped a primrose right into his grasp.

'Now watch that lady in the field turn her penny when she hears my call,' said the cuckoo.

Sam looked to the fields and saw Molly the dairy-maid standing there. When the cuckoo called 'Cuckoo, Cuckoo', in its soft warm beautiful voice Molly bowed her head, dived in her pocket for her money and turned it over. She waved to the cuckoo in the tree. Then she spied Sam sitting close to the cuckoo.

'Was that the cuckoo or Sam Pig?' she asked herself. 'Poor Sam. He seems to be stuck up that tree. I must try to help him.' She hurried back to the farm.

Farmer Greensleeves and Dick came out. They all stared hard at Sam, and the cuckoo flew away. Soon the little pig saw them coming across the fields with a ladder. They set it at the foot of the fir tree, and Sam sighed.

'Come along, Sam. Don't be frightened. We'll get you down,' shouted Dick.

'Don't want to come down,' said Sam.

'Not want? Why, you can't stay there all night! Of course you want to come down,' said Dick, and he scuttled up the ladder.

He popped the little pig under his arm and slowly climbed down, feeling very proud of himself.

Sam could hear the hissing of the ants around him. 'Ss-ss-am-am has come down. Ss-ss-ss-am has-s-s-s come down,' they whispered. 'H-e-e-e cl-cl climbed a t-t-tree,' they told one another and they hissed themselves to bed.

The rain poured down from the cloud, bending the tall tree, shaking every little green needle.

'I'm glad that little pig got down to safety. He would have tumbled in this rain,' said the tree, as it shook its branches and tossed itself in the warm rain.

Sam looked up at the dark cloud and he saw Spring float off and drop to the earth, to sprinkle her flowers over the meadows.

'Spring has come and the cuckoo has come,' he shouted as he ran indoors, wet through but happy. 'I saw the cuckoo and I saw Spring herself.'

'You would,' grunted Tom Pig.

'I did! I did!' shouted Sam. 'Spring gave me this.' He held out the primroses, and they were the sweetest and freshest flowers anyone had ever seen.

A Christmas Tale

As soon as the leaves fell off the trees, Sam Pig began to think of Christmas.

'How long till Christmas, Brock?' he asked.

The badger looked down at the little pig. 'Why do you want to know?'

'Because I am going to make some Christmas presents,' said Sam.

'You've got one more full moon, and when the new moon comes it will be Christmas,' said Brock, looking at his pocket book.

'Brock,' whispered Sam. 'Can you keep a secret?'

'Well, I've kept a few in my time,' said Brock.

'Brock, it's about these Christmas presents.'

'Well, Sam, what about them? Are you thinking about me? Because I should like a new pocket knife with two blades and a corkscrew.'

'No,' stammered Sam, who was quite sure he could never get a pocket knife with two blades for anybody. 'No. I was thinking of giving presents to Farmer Greensleeves and Molly the dairy-maid and Sally the mare and the Alderney cow.'

'Indeed, Sam. You are flying high with no money at all in the world,' said Badger.

'What do human beings like, Brock?' asked Sam.

'I've never been in a house in my life, Sam. You are the adventurer. You had better go to the farm and look through the windows and find out.'

The weather was very cold and Sam ran downstairs in the morning as fast as he could to warm himself by Brock's fire in the kitchen.

'I guess they are cold, too,' said he to himself as he thought of the farmhouse. 'I saw Molly the dairymaid's hands red and chapped with frost.'

'Have you anything for chapped hands, for Molly?' he asked Ann.

'Yes, I made some pots of elder flower salve in the spring,' said Ann. 'I'll give you one for Molly.'

'Oh, thank you, Ann. That's one present ready. I'll go and get some wood for you,' said Sam.

He ran out to gather firewood and as he picked the sticks from the woodland he thought of a present for Mrs Greensleeves. 'I'll take her a bundle of wood, all neat and even,' said he, 'and I'll tie it with a rope of grass ribbon, and decorate it with some pretty fir cones, all ready for their Christmas fire.'

'What about the Alderney cow, and Sally the mare, and Mr Greensleeves? What will you give them?' asked Ann when Sam told her his Christmas hopes and plans.

'I think a nice hat for Sally, made of straw plaited in a circle, with two holes for her ears,' said Sam.

'Yes, I can make that,' agreed Ann, eagerly. 'There is some long straw left from the harvest, and I can twist that, and make a hat and trim it with ears of corn and a few feathers.'

'Rosie the Alderney could have a little shawl to put on her shoulders when the wind is cold,' said Sam, thoughtfully. 'I've seen her look shivery. Can you make a shawl, Ann?'

'Yes,' said Ann. 'I've some sheep's wool in a drawer, and I will make a shawl with it, and fasten it with a thorn-pin.'

So Ann sat down to her weaving and her sewing and her knitting, and brother Sam gave advice and held her wool and threaded her long needles.

'The shady hat will keep the flies off Sally's face and eyes in hot weather,' said Sam happily, as Ann plaited the strands of wheat straw and sewed the plaits in a circle. Then Sam tied a wheat tassel to the brim, and he put a few cock pheasant feathers in the crown. It was a hat fit for a queen, he thought when Ann tried it on. Brock also tried it on, and everyone admired the two holes for Sally's ears.

Then Ann sat at her spinning-wheel and twisted a long thread of sheep's wool ready for her knitting. She knitted a large square, and tied ribbons of wool dyed scarlet to the corners. It was all ready for Rosie the cow.

They set off for the farm on Christmas Eve, carrying their presents. Brock the Badger stayed at home, for he had to look after the fire and watch the mince-pies in the oven.

The four little pigs trotted gaily across the fields, with many a squeak of excitement when one stepped on an ice-covered pool and slid backward, and another stuck in a thorny hedge and a third got stuck in a stile that was too narrow for him. It wasn't easy to go to the farm. They stepped lightly across the yard and Rover snuffled when he heard them.

'A merry Christmas, Rover,' called Sam. 'Oh dear,' he whispered to the others. 'I forgot to get a present for Rover and I love him dearly.'

'I've bones in my pocket,' whispered Bill. 'I was going to play on them, but I'll give them to Rover instead.'

He took the pair of bones to Rover, but they were so smooth, so ivory white, that Rover could not eat them. Instead he played a tune himself, clicking them together.

'I've always wanted to play the bones, Sam,' he called. 'Thank you.'

They called at the cowhouse door and there stood Rosie, half-asleep in the warm building.

'A happy Christmas, Rosie,' said Sam. 'We've brought you a present made by Sister Ann.'

They draped the shawl over her flanks and she mooed with pleasure, wondering what it was.

'It keeps out the draughts,' said she softly. 'There's a little cold wind that comes in to catch me and this keeps me safe from its claws, Sam.'

They went to the stable door where Sally stood dreaming away the hours of Christmas Eve.

'A happy Christmas, Sally,' cried Sam, as he kicked at the door and waited for Sally to draw back the heavy bolt.

'What's this, Sam? A hat? A pretty hat for me? And holes for my ears?' cried Sally, as Sam placed the hat on her head.

'It's really for summer,' explained Sam. 'To keep the flies off your eyes, but it will keep the snow from you in winter.'

'Thank you,' murmured Sally, and she was so surprised that she went on saying, 'Thank you,' all through the night, even when she was asleep.

Farmer Greensleeves sat in the kitchen, listening to the children singing carols, while he ate a large mince-pie.

'Noel, Noel,' sang the children.

'Noel,' came a squeak from the farmyard, and everybody stopped and listened.

'Is it the waits?' they asked. 'Or is it some children from the village?'

They threw open the door, calling, 'Come in, and welcome, whoever you are. Everybody's welcome on Christmas Eve.'

There was silence, and nobody was to be seen.

Then there was a scuffle of little feet, pattering across the cobbles from the darkness and four pink noses were poked in the light, and four pairs of anxious little eyes stared into the kitchen, and four pairs of ears waggled under four drooping hats.

'Oh, it's those pigs,' cried Mrs Greensleeves. 'Well, I never. Fancy coming here on Christmas Eve!'

'A happy Christmas,' called four squeaky voices. 'We have brought you a present, Mrs Greensleeves, for your fire.'

They dropped the faggot of wood with its ribbon of plaited grasses, and its fir cones and holly, on the floor.

'Oh, just what I want,' said Mrs Greensleeves, and she placed the great pile of wood on the fire to make a crackling blaze.

How beautiful it was, with its sparks and serpents and streamers of stars as it hissed and flew up the chimney.

'Come in, all of you,' called Mr Greensleeves.

So they all went into the big farm kitchen, and sat on the floor on the rag hearth-rug. They ate mince-pies and drank warm milk, and sipped a drop of hot elderberry wine, made from the elderberries of the wood.

Molly the dairy-maid came in with a can of milk and when she saw the company she gave a little squeak of alarm.

'Please, Miss Molly,' cried Sam, bowing to her. 'Oh, please, we have brought you some elder-flower salve for your chilblains.'

'Oh, Sam Pig! You kind little pigling! Didn't I tell you, Missis, that Sam is a good fellow?' cried Molly as she took the little wooden bowl filled with the pale green salve.

Then Ann Pig gave Mrs Greensleeves a brass button which she had found in the field, and to Mr Greensleeves she gave a golden guinea which Brock had dug up from the meadow, and to Dick and Mary she gave two little stones with holes through them, which are supposed to bring good luck.

'We'll sing you a carol now,' said Sam. 'Listen, everybody.' So they stood up, with their fists folded before them, and they sang their own little carol.

> *'Christmas comes but once a year,*
> *And when it comes it brings good cheer.*
> *Logs of wood and Christmas cake,*
> *A bucket of milk and a curdy cake.*
> *A kiss and a hug to keep you awake,*
> *And four little pigs to brew and to bake,*
> *On Christmas Day in the morning.'*

The children clapped their hands at this ditty which the little pigs sang in a queer manner, first one singing and then another, and then one repeating and then another, till there was a round of 'curdy cake' and 'keep you awake'.

The children asked for another carol, but Sam did not know another, except a secret one Brock had taught him, too secret to tell anyone, all about the trees and stars and the sky.

So they said goodbye, and away they trooped, carrying a bag full of mincepies and a strange fruit called an orange, and a bucket of milk and some curdy cakes, and a pound of butter and a few eggs. That was a Christmas to remember always, and they thought of it in the blazing summer when Sally wore her straw hat and the flies danced on top of it among the feathers. But Rosie had eaten her shawl long ago, and even Rover had managed to break up and devour his two bones.

A Pinch of Happiness

There was music in the kitchen of the four little pigs. Ann played a tune on the wash-tub, Sam beat the saucepan with a spoon, Bill thumped the tin tray, which was already bent and battered, for Mrs Greensleeves had thrown it away as done for, and Tom clicked a couple of clean bones.

'I've got nothing, you've got nothing, we've got nothing to eat,' they sang, as they banged and clattered their musical instruments.

Then an old beggar-man went past the wood calling: 'Happiness for sale. A penny a pinch, happiness.' He could not see the house, but he could hear the noise. All the little pigs stopped their tunes and went out to buy happiness. He was selling it at a penny a pinch, which was cheap.

'Where does it come from?' asked Sam, tasting his pinch and dancing with joy as it touched his tongue.

'From the tree of Happiness,' grunted the beggar. 'It's for those who have nothing, and sing about nothing.'

'I'll give some to the Fox,' said Sam. 'It may make him better tempered.' He bought another pinch and put it in a nutshell for safety.

They paid for their pinches with some money which lay dirty and dark and bent in the money-box, money which Brock had dug from the ground in a secret place, and he had left it for Sam to wash and scrub and polish. The beggar-man rubbed each coin on his trousers, and some were copper and some were bronze, some were silver and a few were gold. He took them all, but when Brock came home he groaned with sorrow.

'You have given away my store of Roman coins, found in a treasure hoard,' said he sadly. 'But if you got real happiness it is worth it.'

He took a pinch of the happiness himself, and he looked round the room. Everything looked brighter, and the family were all smiling and good.

'Yes, it was worth my silver and gold to get you all so merry,' said he.

Tom and Bill forgot to tease young Sam, Sam offered to wash up and even to clean the saucepan, Ann Pig ran round helping everybody, but Ann was always happy, so the pinch did not make much difference to her.

Sam took his nutshell filled with the powder to find the Fox, but on the way he met a weeping lamb, who had lost her mother.

'Baa-baa,' she sobbed. 'Oh dear. All these sheep

and I can't find my mother and a wolf might eat me.'

'There are no wolves,' said Sam, hurriedly peeping behind him. 'But I'll take you to your mother.' So he boldly entered the flock of sheep, pushing his way between many staring angry ewes, some of whom butted him with their hard heads.

'A motherless lamb. A motherless lamb,' he called, and then he remembered the pinch of happiness. He gave the lamb a taste of the powder, and at once she leapt high on her little black feet, and ran straight to her mother. There was such a cuddling and a baa-ing and tail-wagging as the little creature drank her mother's milk.

'I'm happy,' baa-ed the little lamb.

Sam elbowed his way out of the flock and went to find the Fox. He saw the lithe red creature hurrying across the fields, but the Fox could not stop to speak to him. There was a great commotion, a distant sound, and the sheep were suddenly frightened. They crowded together, and faced one way, as the Fox suddenly turned and dashed among them. In a moment he was hidden from sight except for glimpses of red now and then. The air was filled with hallooing, and a horn blew with a long sweet note, and people called and the hounds bayed. Huntsmen on horseback came galloping over the fields, and the great hounds with lolling tongues bayed as they came after the Fox.

They were very close when the Fox turned into the flock. In the crowd of sheep he was safe, for his scent was lost in the oily smell of the sheep, and the hounds were bewildered as with noses to the ground they searched for him.

He stayed in the great huddle of fleecy animals, and Sam, who was frightened of the hounds, joined him. All round them were sheep and lambs, with startled amber eyes, and pressing bodies.

'Take a pinch of this herb of happiness, Mr Fox,' said Sam, offering the nutshell as if it were a snuff-box. He was sorry for the hard-racing Fox.

'Oh, Sam. Oh, Sam. I am in a state,' panted the Fox, but he took a pinch and at once his breathing became calmer, his eyes lost their fear, and he was strengthened.

'Oh, Sam Pig! That was a close shave. I just got into the flock in the nick of time. Now you've given me a dose of something good. I feel refreshed, I can escape. I have new power, Sam.'

He ran out of the flock on the opposite side, and he dashed into his home wood to take shelter among the rocks. The baying hounds were bewildered and they turned away without him. Then they saw Sam, but they had no power to touch him. He stayed with the sheep and the lambs until the hounds were drawn off by the huntsmen. Then, shaken and happy, he went home.

He gave a pinch of happiness to Sally the mare to

help her in a day of ploughing, and a pinch to Rover the dog. Then he offered a pinch to Dick Green-sleeves, who was dawdling home from school looking rather miserable.

'Hello, Sam Pig,' cried Dick. 'What's this you've got? Are you sure it isn't poison?'

'No, Master Dick. It's right good stuff. A pinch of happiness. I saved the Fox from the hunters with it,' said Sam.

'Save our chickens from the Fox would be better,' said Dick, frowning, but he took a pinch and tasted it.

'A pinch of happiness. I like this,' he cried, and he turned a cart-wheel. 'Yes, I feel all cock-a-hoop. I know how to do my sums, and I remember my Latin, and I've got lots of new ideas. I may pass my examination after all.'

He galloped away, laughing and singing, and Sam met Brock the Badger.

'Oh, Brock,' said he. 'I wish we had a tree of happiness. Then we could taste it as often as we like.'

'No,' said Brock. 'You must never eat too much. The effect is so strong you might get indigestion. Too much happiness is harmful, but a little now and then is very good.'

Brock pointed to some seed flying in the air, fluttering like the parachutes of dandelions, shining like silver as the wind carried them along out of reach.

'Anyone can find a bit of happiness blowing about in the air, if he just stands and stares,' said Brock.

'Where?' asked Sam.

'See, it is flying over there. Look at the flowers and birds and the stars and moon, and you are surely certain to see a few seeds of happiness floating by, and if you open your mouth wide, a seed may fly in.'

Brock laughed and Sam laughed too, and away they went, looking at all the things of earth spread out before them, and tasting again the seeds of happiness, which every little animal and many a child knows how to find.

The Orchestra

Sam heard the music one afternoon in winter as he went home after a visit to Sally the mare.

'I'll just step through the village, Sally,' he said. 'There's something going on and I want to find out what it is.'

He stretched up and tickled Sally's nose and the mare moved her head up and down with enjoyment. It was cold and an icy wind blew over the fields. Sally's hair was thick, she had grown her winter coat, but Sam's coat was thin and he had forgotten his muffler. He shivered a little and drew closer to his large warm friend.

'How do you know there's something on?' asked Sally.

'There was a paper notice on the door,' said Sam. 'It wasn't an exciting notice with pictures of lions and elephants on it, like a circus. Oh, Sally, do you 'member that circus?'

'I do indeed,' said Sally. 'I nearly lost my friend Sam Pig. He nearly joined that circus.'

'Sometimes I wish ... I wish ...' began Sam

dreamily as he thought of the fairy girl riding on a horse.

'Tell me what was on that notice,' interrupted Sally, sternly.

'No pictures, nothing but letters. I couldn't read it although I am good at reading. Long words, Sally. Hard words.'

Sally waited patiently. She was used to waiting.

'I couldn't read a word, Sally, but I heard a woman talking about it. She said it was a 'kestra playing music, such as we never have in our village.'

'Then she has never heard you playing your fiddle, or squeaking on the gate,' observed Sally slyly.

'This 'kestra! What is it?' asked Sam.

'Some kind of bird,' said Sally. 'Can't be a kestrel, Sam, it doesn't sing. You're mistook.'

'No, Sally. She said 'kestra,' said Sam, nodding his head in emphasis. ' 'Twas Mrs Bunting from the shop. She sells cakes and bullseyes, Sally. She said she was getting the tea for the folk who would go to hear that 'kestra play.'

'It's a puzzlement,' said Sally. 'I've heard nothing so I am sure Farmer Greensleeves isn't going.'

They both turned as Farmer Greensleeves came across the field towards them.

'So long, Sam,' said Sally. 'It's my bedtime. I'm off to my warm stable, and you'd best go home to your warm kitchen.'

'So long, Sally,' answered Sam. 'I'll look in at the village hall first to see this 'kestra. I feel like a bit of adventure before I go to bed.'

Farmer Greensleeves took Sally by the forelock to lead her away, but he had a word with Sam.

'Evening, Sam,' said he, cheerfully. 'Cold night. You be off home where all good pigs should be.'

'Master, I'm going to peep at this 'kestra,' piped Sam.

''Kestra? Oh, you mean orchestra. It's in the village hall now, playing to the people who have money to spend and time to listen,' said the farmer. 'I've neither time nor money, and it's not for the likes of you, either, Sam Pig.'

Sam hurried away whispering to himself. 'He doesn't know. I might like that 'kestra. I'm musical myself.'

He ran swiftly through the fields and along the narrow lane to the village. There he went warily. The lamps in the market place were not lit; there were only a few children playing Hop-Scotch and Sam kept in the shadows out of their way. Mrs Bunting's shop had a candle burning to keep out the frost.

Across the village green was the hall which Sam regarded with interest. Instead of being in darkness a yellow light shone from the long, narrow windows and music came floating in the air. Sam scuttled near and stood under a window.

'Fiddles and fiddle-de-dees. Lots of lovely squeaks,' said he, excitedly, and he pricked both his ears to listen and leapt up and down. 'It's more noise than me and Ann and all of us together can make. It's nice music, very high, very squeaky, very quick but good.'

He smacked his lips as if he could eat it, and he shivered with joy and excitement at the beautiful tunes coming from the violins.

'Lots of fiddles like mine. I must look in at them and see this hawk-kestra,' whispered Sam. He glanced round and he saw a pair of steps left outside by the caretaker who had been arranging the room. Quickly he climbed up. The music soared around him; sometimes it seemed to come from the bare trees overhead and sometimes from the sky where the first star was shining down at Sam.

He gazed into the room at a group of people on a small platform with violins and 'cello and flute, and a very select audience which sat enraptured before them on stiff, wooden chairs. They were listening to the last item in the programme.

'Big fiddle, middle-sized fiddle and flute, but never a little magical fiddle like mine,' thought Sam.

Then he noticed a lady at a piano at the side of the platform and he nearly fell in his efforts to watch her nimble fingers. 'It's like playing a tune on the wooden palings,' he murmured. 'Take a stick and run up and down.'

The music was so entrancing Sam could not hold out any longer. He quite forgot where he was. He raised his nose in the air, he gazed at the soft, blue sky where a new moon was sending a radiance and the evening star glowed.

> '*Hey diddle diddle, play her a tune,*
> *Play on the fiddle, sing to the moon,*'

warbled Sam. At the same moment a donkey on the village green began to bray, 'Hee-haw, hee-haw.' Then there was a commotion in the room. One of the ladies in the orchestra saw Sam's little pink face raised to the sky, she heard that wailing cry and the donkey's bray. Her bow slipped and she, too, made a squeak like a dying balloon. People sprang to their feet, the violins stopped and everybody looked in Sam's direction.

Sam started in a fright, he lost his balance and tumbled down. He scrambled to his feet and rushed away just as the door of the hall opened and a man came out. Sam didn't stop to explain, panic seized him as he flew on his stout little feet down the village street, through a cottage garden into the fields.

'One of the village children making a noise,' explained the secretary, apologizing for the interruption. 'They're not used to an orchestra.'

'A very ugly child,' said the lady who had seen Sam most clearly. 'More like a pig than a boy, but you never can tell nowadays.' The concert proceeded but the secretary wrote a note of protest to the village schoolmistress about the behaviour of her children. Sam Pig, unconscious of this, was on his way home.

'Beautiful moon, beautiful moon,' he warbled, and the Fox, who was waiting for a fat rabbit, sprang on the little unsuspecting pig and boxed his ears.

'Why must you always sing when I'm hunting?' he barked.

''Cos I heard some music at the 'kestra,' sobbed Sam, rubbing his sore head. 'You needn't have hit me so hard, Mr Fox.'

He went along more quietly after that, but before he got home he had recovered and he began to sing as he thought of his fiddle and all the tunes he would play.

Brock was smoking by the fire. He wore his carpet slippers embroidered with roses and he had a woollen cap on his head, not to keep out the cold, but because he hid his box of matches there, safe from all the little pigs.

'Brock,' cried Sam, rushing into the room and knocking over a bowl of hot soup which Tom held.

'Look where you're going,' growled Tom crossly.

'Brock,' cried Sam. 'I've heard a 'kestra and seen a 'kestra playing fiddles in the village hall. No children, only ladies all playing fiddles.'

'Really, Sam?' asked Brock, smiling.

'It was lovely, Brock,' stammered Sam, excitedly. 'It was nearly like the wind and the rain and the trees crying in a storm. I want us to be a 'kestra, Brock, four of us playing fiddles and one stroking the palings round the stackyard with a stick.'

'I'm not going to play the fiddle,' said Tom and Bill at once.

'Nobody asked you,' replied Sam, sharply. 'I shall play the fiddle because I've got one. Brock will play the – what do you play, Brock?'

'I have a flute hidden away on the shelf,' said Brock amiably. 'I made it from an elder cutting. I'll tootle my flute. Always ready to oblige a little pig when he is polite.'

'I'll play the drum,' said Tom. 'I can manage the kettle-drum.' He banged the copper kettle with a poker. A lovely deep ring came from it. They listened as Tom played a rattling march which set their heels drumming too.

'What about you, Bill?' said Sam.

'I'll play the bones,' replied Bill. 'I've always wanted to play the bones.'

'Whose bones?' asked Sam anxiously.

'Whose? Why yours, dear Sam,' answered Bill. 'Your nice little bones are well covered with fat, but you might spare a couple for me to rattle together. Two from your legs would do.'

He pinched Sam's legs to find the bones.

'Oh no,' cried Sam. He was rather frightened, but Brock chuckled.

'He's only joking,' said Brock. 'The bones Bill will play are two bones he dug up and he flips them to make a tune.'

'Then we shall have a real 'kestra,' smiled Sam. 'For Ann can play the triangle instead of the palings. We can't carry palings about with us.'

He climbed on a chair to lift down his little fiddle which hung from a hook in the ceiling. He put in a new string made from a fine wire which he had found on the farm. He tuned it and stroked it, and he resined the bow with a knob of hard resin from a spruce tree in the wood. Drops of resin lie on the scaly bark in the spring and Sam always collects them to keep for his fiddle bow. He played a wild little air, and Tom banged on the kettle, Bill clicked his bones, Ann tinkled her triangle and Brock fluted on his elder pipe.

'A real 'kestra,' said Sam, with satisfaction.

After supper Brock told an old story of a magical fiddle which set everybody dancing – the blacksmith with his red-hot horseshoe, the miller with his sack of flour, the farmer with his horse, the baker with his basket of bread. They all jigged until they had to beg for mercy.

'That's what I did once with a leprechaun's shoe,' said Sam, wistfully.

'Let's take our 'kestra and play at the farm,' suggested Ann, her face pink with excitement as she tinkled on her triangle.

'Yes, let's go tomorrow night and play to Sally,' said Sam. 'She likes music and she's never heard a 'kestra. Farmer Greensleeves might like it too.'

'I'm not so sure,' answered Brock. 'I think you must excuse me. He wouldn't be pleased to see me even with a flute. You must go alone. A quartette instead of a quintette.'

The pigs were puzzled by his grand words but Brock told them it meant four playing instead of five.

'What shall we play?' asked Sam. Brock stroked his black and white face and thought for a few minutes.

'"Serenade for Sally" is a good title. That means it's music for one you love.'

'I can easily do that,' said Sam, joyfully, and he played a cascade of notes like a waterfall, although Bill said it was more like a kettle boiling over.

'You, Bill and Tom and Ann have only to tinkle and bang and rattle. I play the real 'kestra music,' boasted Sam, proudly waving his bow.

'Quiet,' said Brock. 'Off to bed at once.'

All the next day they practised their music and at night they got ready, for Sam said a real 'kestra played when the stars came out.

Sam washed his face and put on his Sunday scarf. Ann draped a striped blanket round her shoulders to keep herself warm. Tom wore a red waistcoat and carried the poker ready to bang on any kettle or door that might be ready for his drum music. Bill wore a thick coat of Brock's which had a piece cut off the bottom so that it fitted the little pig. Brock was staying at home to take care of the fire. He said he had some work to do while they were away.

The Badger smiled at the little 'kestra setting off with its musical instruments. Sam carried a lantern, and Ann had a candle in a brass candlestick. Tom said his poker would beat the drum or beat the enemies whoever they were. Bill said he would rattle anybody's bones together for two pins.

They went to the farm and stepped gently across the farmyard, for they did not want to disturb Farmer Greensleeves. A light shone under the kitchen door and through the farm windows they could see Farmer Greensleeves sitting in an armchair reading his newspaper, Mrs Greensleeves darning and the children reading their books. Rover, the dog, never barked, for Sam whispered before he opened the gate.

'Hush, sh-sh, Rover. It's only me, Sam Pig, and the rest of us,' murmured Sam.

'What do you want?' growled Rover.

'We've come to serenade Sally,' said Sam. 'We're a 'kestra all playing a serenade.'

'Never heard of such a thing,' muttered Rover, and he went into his kennel.

They went to the stable door and Sam climbed up and unfastened the top half. Sally turned her head in surprise and alarm.

'What's the matter? Anything wrong?' she asked.

'We've come to play "Serenade for Sally",' whispered Sam, and before Sally could say anything he began. Ann tinkled her triangle as fast as she could so that it sounded like an alarm clock. Bill rattled the pair of bones with all his might, Tom drummed on the stable door and Sam played the fiddle. He forgot all about the fountain of music which he had composed. He forgot all the lovely tunes in his haste to get in front of the others. It was a musical race, with Sam's bow running up and down pouring out the notes, wrong notes and right notes, thin notes and fat notes, high notes and low notes, while tinkling triangle, the rattling bones and the drumming door accompanied the sound.

The door of the farmhouse opened and a voice shouted out, 'What's going on? Who's making that noise? It's Bedlam let loose.'

'Please, Master, it's Sam Pig's 'kestra; we're serenading Sally,' called Sam, and on he raced trying to catch up with his fiddle.

'Stop!' roared the farmer. 'What do you think you're playing?'

'"Serenade for Sally",' replied Sam meekly.

'Well, be off! Sally doesn't want any serenading,'

said the farmer crossly. 'You're waking up the whole farm.'

Mrs Greensleeves whispered to her husband and he came across to the little group of disconsolate players. His frown had gone.

'Missus says I'm to ask you to come to the door,' said he. 'She wants to see this 'kestra.'

The little company trotted across the cobbles to the side-door. Mrs Greensleeves looked at their shining faces and their bright eyes. Then she fetched a plate of currant buns and a basket of apples from the larder.

'Take these, you poor little creatures,' said she. 'You meant well, I'm sure. It was very nice music. Thank you all.'

The little pigs were so surprised at this from Mrs Greensleeves they stammered and bowed, but Sam remembered his manners and thanked Mrs Greensleeves very sweetly.

'Shall we play Serenade to you?' he asked. So Sam played the tune he had made up the night before, all about the wind in the trees and the birds in the air, and Mrs Greensleeves loved it.

'Tell me, Sam,' said Mr Greensleeves, 'was it you who frightened the orchestra in the village last night?'

'I 'specks so,' said Sam, grinning. 'I looked in at the window and sang a bit.'

'I thought it was you. I said "That was Sam Pig,

that was" when I heard, but nobody would believe me. The secretary complained to the schoolteacher and she scolded the children and asked who had done it. Our Mary and Dick thought it might be you, but I was certain sure it was.'

'It was beautiful music the 'kestra played,' said Sam. 'I liked it so much I wanted to play the same.'

'Yes, of course,' murmured Mrs Greensleeves.

'Well, good night, all of you. I'll shut Sally's door and you must go home,' said Farmer Greensleeves.

'Good night, Master. Good night, Missus. Good night, Sally and Rover,' called the little pigs and very contentedly they trotted home with their basket of buns and apples.

'I'm going to compose a new serenade tomorrow,' said Sam solemnly. 'I shall make some water music and call it "Serenade to a Fish". I shall play it down by the river and perhaps a water-maid may peep at me and fishes may come up ready for Ann's frying pan.' All the way home he invented his new serenade.

When they got to the house Brock was still busy but he listened to their story of adventure. Then he showed them what he had been making.

'I'm making a 'kestra for you,' said he. 'It is called an Aeolian Harp because it is a harp for the wind himself to play.'

'Like the harp the mermaid plays in the river?' asked Sam, as he looked at the strip of wood with

long, fine wires fastened tightly across to make harp
strings.

'Not quite, Sam. This makes orchestral music like
many fiddles and harps playing together. The wind
will touch it with its fingers and play to you.' Brock
finished the wind harp and hung it on the window-
sill in a narrow crack so that the wind could catch
the strings as it passed in and out of the room. They
all sat down to supper but the wind didn't come.
Sam played his tune to Brock and they forgot about
the Aeolian Harp as they laughed and sang together.

However, in the night they were all wakened by
the lovely music made by the fingers of the wind. It
was music of trees and birds and fairyland and
magic. It was the most beautiful music in the world
and only the wind's orchestra could play it.

Red Shoes

One day Sam Pig was rootling among the dead leaves of a hedge when he found a pair of shoes. They were not like your shoes or mine. No, not at all! They were a pair of pig-shoes, made of scarlet leather. At first Sam thought they were scarlet toadstools growing there, and he picked them up to put in his basket of truffles and other toadstools. He looked at them again and he saw they were shoes. He tried them on, and they fitted him perfectly. They might have been made for him. Indeed they had, if he had known. He ran home in them and showed them to sister Ann.

'Oh, lovely shoes!' cried Ann. 'Do let me try them on. We take the same size, Sam.'

But when Ann took the little shoes her small feet would not go into them. The shoes fell off like dried leaves, so it was evident they belonged to Sam.

The shoes took charge of Sam. They took him to the woods when he wished to go in the opposite direction. If he set off for the fields, then the shoes would lead him to a shady lane. He came to the farm when he went out to pick up sticks. He went through the village when it was not really safe.

It was no use for Sam to struggle with his shoes, and if he did not want to go their way then he had to remove them and hang them round his neck, when they kicked him with little prods. All the same, he loved his red shoes, which were so soft and comfortable and so queer.

One day they led him, protesting as usual, through the village to a field where he had never been before, a dangerous field with people in it.

'Look here, shoes,' said Sam. 'Look, I don't like this place, and I would rather not go here if you don't mind.'

The shoes bustled him through the gate into the field where there were many boys, and white lines and great pieces of wood. The shoes stopped by a wooden house with steps and Sam went up. He would have run away but the shoes kept him firmly on.

'Here's another of them, late, of course,' said a boy, looking out. 'Here's the eleventh man, late.'

Sam entered the bare room, bewildered by the boys in their football shirts.

'Come along. Hurry up!' cried one. 'The whistle will blow in a minute. We've been waiting for you.'

So Sam hustled into the changing-room, and then somebody noticed his red shoes.

'Just look at his boots,' said he.

'Oh, they belong to a well-known club, I think,' said another boy. Sam nodded his head and kept his mouth shut. He was pushed out of doors with a stream of boys, to the field. Although he longed to take to his heels, he couldn't. Indeed the shoes seemed more firmly fixed than ever and he looked down to see that they had grown longer, they encased his ankles, they had red laces, they were padded.

A football came bouncing out of the pavilion, and Sam's eyes sparkled. He had always wanted one of those things.

'Put red shoes in goal,' said somebody, and he was pushed towards the goal, where he felt safe.

Then the whistle blew and the game began. Sam danced up and down in the goal, waiting for the ball, which flew overhead from one to another. At last, at last, there was a surge his way, and the ball was shot towards him. His red shoes took possession and they leapt forward. The shoes kicked as if they had been waiting all their lives for this moment. The ball soared away, far away, up in the air, and away out of the ground. Sam ran after it, and everyone yelled to him, but he took no notice, for the shoes would not wait.

He caught the ball and went on kicking it, up the lane, through the village across the fields and the wood, until he got home.

After him streamed the angry boys, but they had

to give up. They lost sight of Sam as he ran through the woods.

'I've got a football, all my own,' he shouted as the ball entered the house and he came after it.

'Now, Sam,' said Brock mildly. 'What's this? You've taken a football from the village, but you must send it back at once. It isn't yours, Sam.'

'It belongs to my red shoes,' said Sam.

'You kick it back again, Sam. I will make you a football for your red shoes,' said Brock.

So Sam took the ball across the field to the edge of the village. Then he gave a great kick, and the ball flew so high he couldn't see it. It flew over the village, over the church, over the blacksmith's shop, right to the turret of the village school, where it set the bell a-ringing. There the children found it and then took it away to play with again. There were two little red imprints on it, and it was the best football ever known after this. Even a little kick sent it soaring, as if it remembered the touch of the little red shoes.

But Sam went slowly home, for the shoes were reluctant to turn back. Then Brock showed him the new football. It was made of air-bubbles, enclosed in a cover of swirling vapours of many rainbow colours. It floated like a soap bubble, as Brock gave it to Sam.

The red shoes and Sam took it out to the common. Sam gave it a kick and it went high in the air. It kept

rising, until it was like a far-away bubble, with light shining from it. The shoes and Sam stood looking after it. Then the shoes struggled free from Sam and they too hovered in the air. Sam gave them a kick, for he was weary of them. They flew up and followed the ball. Like the earth and her planet the moon they orbited, circling round the earth, shining like a silvery globe, and two scarlet shoes following after for ever.

'A new star,' said the astronomers, as they looked at this strange shining orb through their telescopes. 'Red as Mars.'

'It's my football with my red shoes following it,' said Sam, but nobody in the village believed that tale.

The Thief

There was a great talk in the woods and fields. A robber had crept out in the night and stolen Badger's flute, the special flute he had made from an elder tree. It was hanging on the wall and now it had gone. Everybody looked for the thief. Footprints were examined in the garden, but, of course, with four little pigs running all over the place and many birds and wild animals, it was nearly impossible to find prints among them. The sheet of horn which covered the window instead of glass had been pushed up at the corner to allow somebody to enter. It wasn't man for his footmarks were well known. Man clumped about in big boots. It wasn't a wolf either or a bear. Who could it be?

Ann Pig set the breakfast, five plates of porridge and five bowls of milk. Then she went to the larder to find a tin of treacle. Sam Pig was down the garden staring at the sky, listening to the clouds. Brock the Badger was feeling the wind and sniffing the air. Tom the cook was standing at the fire with his back to the room toasting the bread. Bill was leaning over the gate. When Ann Pig came back to the kitchen there was nothing on the table, every drop of milk and porridge had gone.

'It's a clever thief,' said Brock. 'It's someone who knows our ways.'

The birds were all talking to one another, speaking of the thief who had entered the house of the four pigs and Brock the Badger. A robin said he knew who it was. It was a cat-burglar. He had seen a cat wandering in the woods, a tabby cat, striped like a tiger and its eyes were green and its teeth sharp.

'A cat-burglar,' said everybody, and there was such a chattering and such a hiss, so many cries of alarm from the blackbirds, so many warnings from the smaller birds, that everybody was on the alert.

Now the cat was hiding in the barn, ready to return when the talking had died down. She came out in the evening, stepping softly in the shadows, crawling on her stomach through the woods, taking little leaps over brambles, speeding behind the trees when anyone looked her way. She returned to the house of the four pigs and looked through the window. There was a bowl of milk and some fish; her eyes sparkled and she gently swished her long, striped tail.

Then the watching birds gave their alarm and the little pigs sprang to their feet and rushed out of doors. The trees murmured but they did not say where the cat lay, for trees are neutral in the struggle for life. They stood serene and beautiful, waving their boughs and sheltering the cat with their moving shadows.

The squirrel spied her and threw nuts at her, chattering angrily. The hedgehogs down below spread out their prickles, made themselves into balls and grunted like old men. The snakes hissed and the ants stammered their cries, the mice squeaked and the rats squealed.

Then Brock the Badger stepped forward and cried out to the cat. 'Come forth, O Cat,' he commanded, and the cat came from her shelter.

'Why do you steal from us who have been your friends?' asked Brock sternly.

'Because I am hungry,' said the cat.

'You belong to man. He should feed you,' said Brock. 'You are not wild.'

'I have left man,' said the cat. 'Nobody wants me. My kittens were drowned and I am unhappy.'

'Give me back my flute,' said Brock, and the cat dropped the flute from the tree.

'I like music,' said she; 'people throw things at me when I sing, so I stole your flute to play instead.'

'I know who would take care of you,' said Sam Pig. 'The old Witch-woman wants a cat like you. She doesn't want a tame cat but one that is rather wild so that she can let it hunt and she can talk to it on winter nights, for all witch-women have cats.'

So the wild cat went to the Witch-woman and

there it was welcomed. She buttered its feet so that it would not stray, and she sang little songs to the cat in her high cracked voice, and the cat sang back to her. Gradually it became a tame cat, for she was so full of kindness and love the cat could not harm her. It stayed by her fire and slept in her house and it no longer went out to thieve in the woods. So there was peace again in the wild wood.

The Wishing-Bird

One day Sam found a bird's nest. He was walking down the lane in the spring sunshine keeping close to the hedge and rustling his toes in the white violets and cowslips when he caught sight of a bird's nest. Of course Sam had often discovered nests, for his eyes were quick and he spent most of his time out of doors, but birds were friends of his and he never harmed any of the little creatures of the air which flew so lightly overhead. He left their nests alone, lest man should find them, for all the animals were afraid of man.

This nest was different; it was unlike any nest Sam had ever seen. It was very small, only the size of an egg-cup. It was lined with hair and grass and fringed with moss, and little ferns were woven in the side of it, with two or three blue feathers for ornaments.

Was it the nest of the chaffinch, a clever and original chaffinch? 'Spink, spink,' called Sam, enticingly. He raised himself up the bank to look into the nest, but no bird was there. He felt very carefully within and brought out four tiny eggs, as blue as the sky and as bright as glass. They were cold.

'What a foolish bird to leave her eggs like this,' thought Sam. 'These will never hatch out now. I will take them home to Brock.'

So, dancing on his way, he went through the fields and he soon forgot all about the little eggs which lay in his pocket. He saw something else, shining white jewels in the grass, and he rushed to look closer.

'Mushrooms for tea. The first mushrooms,' he cried joyfully, as he knelt to gather them. They were like little silky umbrellas waiting for a fairy to use them. He grunted with pleasure as he pulled each one carefully. He did not put them in his pocket, that might have crushed them. No, he pulled a wisp of hay from a haystack in the corner of the field and twisted a little nest and put the small mushrooms carefully inside so that the pink gills should not be harmed.

'Mushrooms for tea,' he sang as he went up the garden path.

> '*One, two, three, mushrooms for tea.*
> *One for Ann and one for me,*
> *One for Brock and one for me,*
> *One for Tom and little Bill-ee.*'

'Oh, lovely mushrooms,' cried Ann, clapping her hands. 'Clever Sam to find them and to bring them home in a nest.'

Sam peeled them and cooked them in a saucer with a lump of butter and a spoonful of cream. That is the old country way to cook mushrooms fresh from the fields. The little pigs sat round the table and Brock the Badger served out to each a portion of the dark, grey mushrooms and the thick, creamy gravy, smelling like the earth itself.

'Thank you, Sam, for finding such a treasure,' said Brock kindly, and Sam blushed with pride, for such praise was not often given.

'I found something else,' said he, suddenly remembering. 'In a nest.' He fumbled in his pocket and brought out the four glass marbles.

'Whose eggs are these?' asked Tom. 'Take 'em back.'

'They were cold,' protested Sam.

Each little pig grabbed an egg and shook it and licked it in wonder. The eggs were hard as stone.

'What kind of bird flew off the nest?' asked Brock.

'No bird at all,' said Sam. 'I called and nobody came.'

Brock rose and went to the shelf where he kept his brown note-book with the knowledge of badgers, the ancient folk of the earth itself. He turned the ragged parchment pages of the old, worn book, and the four pigs watched him eagerly. When Brock consulted this book there was something special afoot.

'Is it an unknown bird?' asked Sam. 'Is it rare?'

'I rather think so,' said Brock quietly. 'I believe those eggs were laid by a wishing-bird. It is a green bird and it makes a pretty nest, and it lays eggs with wishes inside them, not little birds.'

'Wishes! Wishes!' cried Sam. 'Can we have the wishes?'

'Yes, you can have them,' said Brock slowly, and he looked round at the startled eyes and the excited faces of the four little pigs. 'You can have them, but you must do something in return.'

'What?' asked Sam. 'What can we do?'

'I don't know,' replied Brock, simply. 'It's not in the book.'

'What shall I wish for?' asked Ann, clasping her little egg.

'What would you like to see?' asked Brock, smiling at her.

'A tiger-lily,' said Ann. 'I've never seen one.'

She squeezed her egg and there was a sharp explosion and the egg fell apart. Out of it grew a tiny golden flower which expanded quickly, growing taller until it reached the ceiling. There stood a great gold and flame tiger-lily, spotted and beautiful. They all stared in delight, and Ann touched the leaves with her little paws.

'My own tiger-lily,' said she, relieved to see it was a flower and not a fierce tiger.

Sam, Tom and Bill were all thinking of their wishes but they didn't want flowers. Something much more exciting must come to them, they decided.

'I want a pony,' said Tom and the egg cracked and out stepped a tiny pony small as a bumble bee. It had minute shaggy feet and a smooth face and a long mane like feathers. At once it began to grow. It whinnied gently and it kicked its heels. Brock led it outside, for the kitchen was no place for a pony. It had golden hoofs and a flowing tail and it frisked on the grass. Then Tom got on its back and rode off to the woods.

They could hear the sound of the pony's hoofs and Tom's voice as he talked to his treasure. Then the sounds died away and there was only the crackle of the bracken.

'I wish Sally could see that pony,' said Sam.

'It's your turn, Bill,' said Brock the Badger, giving Bill his egg.

Bill held it a long time, considering. Then he made a strange wish.

'I wish to have a bear,' said he. 'A tame bear,' he added in a sudden panic.

The egg cracked and out came a tiny, brown bear as small as a cobnut, shaggy and good-tempered. It grew and grew, from a nice little bear-cub to a large brown bear. Bill yelled with terror and delight, but he took a bit of honeycomb and fed the beast. As it ate the honey the bear grew. It stood on its hind legs and stared round with small golden eyes. Brock

slipped a rope round its neck and led it through the door into the garden.

Bill followed in some fear but he took the rope and the two of them went into the woods.

Ann had run upstairs and Sam was behind Brock.

'Oh dear, I do hope it won't eat Farmer Green-sleeves' cows,' said Sam. 'Why did Bill ask for a bear?'

'I hope it won't eat Bill,' said Ann. She put her arm round her lily and the yellow pollen fell on her head. 'I'm glad I had a lily,' said she.

'Now, Sam, what about your wish?' asked Brock.

'I want to see a wishing-bird,' said Sam. 'I ask for a little wishing-bird to come out of the egg.'

The last egg cracked and out flew a very tiny bird, not much bigger than a lady-bird. It grew quickly and then it spread its wings and settled on Sam's hands like a butterfly.

It was green and blue, with green wings and blue feathers on its breast and a gold crest on its blue head. It preened itself and then it sang a sweet, warbling song. At once there was a flutter of wings and the mother wishing-bird came out of the sky.

'Oh, my little young child,' sang the wishing-bird. 'This is what I have always longed for. Nobody ever thought of me, doomed to give wishes to others and never having the happiness of a little songster of my own.'

The two birds circled round one another and flew up and down the room singing happily.

'Thank you, Sam Pig,' said the wishing-bird. 'You have delivered me from that spell which made me lay wishing eggs for others and never for myself.' Then they rose in the air and flew away. They went across the seas to their own country, where they met birds of their kind and there they lived for ever.

As darkness came down Tom Pig returned from his ride in the woods. He was tired and bed-raggled.

'Where's the pony?' asked Brock.

'Oh, he galloped on and on and suddenly he changed into smoke. He completely disappeared like the mists in the wood. I have been walking back ever since.'

Then Bill came back without his bear and he had a similar tale to tell.

'My bear ran along and I kept hold of the rope. After a time he became shadowy and then he faded away. I was left holding the rope with nothing on it. He was an invisible bear, so I came home.'

But Ann's tiger-lily kept its beauty and after a week or two Sam Pig took it to Mrs Greensleeves to plant in her garden, where it grew for many a year.

'We had some fun with our wishes,' said Sam, when they talked about the wishing-bird.

'Your wish set the wishing-bird free,' said Ann. 'I expect there are lots of wishing-birds now from all the eggs they will lay.'

'And we might have a wish just by seeing them fly over.'

About the author

Alison Uttley was born in 1887 in Derbyshire, and was brought up on a farm some distance from a village, which meant she dwelt in a real solitude of fields and woods. She was never lonely – she had calves, lambs, foals, dogs, and her small brother for companions, as well as country people, the hedger, the ditcher, Irish haymakers and the oatcake man.

She won a scholarship to a small grammar school, and although her chief interest was music, she turned to mathematics and science and went to Manchester University, gaining a degree in Physics Honours. After going to Cambridge for a year, where she studied English with pleasure and surprise, she taught science at a London school, then married a civil engineer and had a son.

The child listened eagerly to her stories, which she had secretly been writing in an attic, and she finally sent one to a publisher, who made a book of it and asked for more, to her astonishment. Since then her animal characters Little Grey Rabbit, Hare, Squirrel, Sam Pig, Brock the Badger, Tim Rabbit, Brown Mouse, Little Red Fox have been compared with the creations of Beatrix Potter.

Mrs Uttley died in May 1976.

Some other Young Puffins

Joseph's Bear

Evelyn Davies

The bear was the very best thing that Joseph had ever owned, but when you love something you may have to make a hard decision.

Stories for Five-year-olds
Stories for Six-year-olds
Stories for Seven-year-olds
Stories for Eight-year-olds

ed. Sara and Stephen Corrin

Celebrated anthologies of stories specially selected for each age group and tested in the classroom by the editors.

The Elephant Party and Other Stories

Paul Biegel

What is the connexion between a circus elephant and a pink pudding? How could a teapot make a mouse lose her fears and a king hop on one leg? The most unlikely things seem quite natural in this collection of fantastic tales.

Where Matthew Lives

Teresa Verschoyle

Happy stories about a little boy exploring his new home, a cottage tucked away by the sea. (*Original*)

Tales of Joe and Timothy
Joe and Timothy Together

Dorothy Edwards

Friendly, interesting stories about two small boys living in
different flats in a tall, tall house, and the good times they
have together.

The Bus Under the Leaves

Margaret Mahy

Adam didn't even like David, until they began playing in
the old bus that made such a wonderful hideout, and soon they
were the best of friends.

Bandicoot and His Friends

Violet Philpott

Lion promised his friends a surprise when he came home from
India, but no one expected anything half as nice as friendly,
funny, furry little Bandicoot, who was so kind and clever when
any of his friends were in trouble.

Umbrella Thursday and A Helping Hand

Janet McNeill

Good deeds sometimes have funny results, as the two little
girls in these stories discover.

Candy Floss and Impunity Jane

Rumer Godden

Two stories about dolls by an author who understands their
feelings.